Prisoner of the Levant

World Writing in French
A Winthrop-King Institute Series

Series Editors
Charles Forsdick (University of Liverpool)
and
Martin Munro (Florida State University)

Advisory Board Members
Jennifer Boum Make (Georgetown University)
Michelle Bumatay (Florida State University)
William Cloonan (Florida State University)
Michaël Ferrier (Chuo University)
Michaela Hulstyn (Stanford Univesity)
Khalid Lyamlahy (University of Chicago)
Helen Vassallo (University of Exeter)

There is a growing interest among Anglophone readers in literature in translation, including contemporary writing in French in its richness and diversity. The aim of this new series is to publish cutting-edge contemporary French-language fiction, travel writing, essays and other prose works translated for an English-speaking audience. Works selected will reflect the diversity, dynamism, originality, and relevance of new and recent writing in French from across the archipelagoes – literal and figurative – of the French-speaking world. The series will function as a vital reference point in the area of contemporary French-language prose in English translation. It will draw on the expertise of its editors and advisory board to seek out and make available for English-language readers a broad range of exciting new work originally published in French. This series is published in partnership with the Winthrop-King Institute, Florida State University.

Darina Al Joundi

Prisoner of the Levant

Translated by Helen Vassallo

Liverpool University Press

First published in English translation by Liverpool University Press 2024
Liverpool University Press
4 Cambridge Street
Liverpool
L69 7ZU

Prisoner of the Levant was first published in French as *Prisonnière du Levant*
© Éditions Grasset & Fasquelle, 2017

British Library Cataloguing-in-Publication data
A British Library CIP record is available

ISBN 978-1-80207-875-6 hardback
ISBN 978-1-80207-874-9 paperback

Typeset by Carnegie Book Production, Lancaster
Printed and bound by CPI Group (UK) Ltd, Croydon CR0 4YY

For May: thank you

I place a mirror facing yours
For you to be eternal.
Ahmad Shamlou

I

May was born on 11th February 1886, and I was born on 25th February 1968. Our paths could never have crossed. And yet my life has always been bound to hers. My first encounter with May was in a class on Arab literature. The teacher was telling us about a woman who used to hold one of Cairo's greatest literary salons. She was a journalist, and was the love of Khalil Gibran's life.

As a child, I liked to spend time alone, especially at my aunt's house. She lived in Hazmiyeh, a fashionable suburb that overlooks Beirut. Her garden backed onto another building, an old and very grand one. I used to jump over the low stone wall that separated us from that building. Then I'd walk through its gardens, which were full of tired-looking women wearing white dresses.

It was there that May had been shut away and, years later, it was in a place just like it that my family shut me away.

I was released when a large television channel wanted me to play the lead role in their big new show. The filming was intense, we filmed dozens of episodes at a time. Whenever there was a break in filming, I would go up onto the terrace that overlooked the bay. I'd drink a cup of coffee and smoke a cigarette and stare off at an old building up in the nearby hills. It had a beautiful balcony that also looked out on the bay. When I asked who owned the apartment with the balcony, I was told:

'It belonged to Ameen Rihani, and next to it is the one where May Ziadeh stayed after she was released from the asylum'.

It seemed that everything was leading me towards May.

After I was discharged from the asylum, I couldn't come to terms with what my family had done to me. I couldn't fathom how it was possible that I ended up in a place like that. The image of it was unbearable to me, and my memory blocked it out. The people around me, their voices, their laughter, the way they behaved towards me, it was all so violent. Alone and exhausted, I slept with one eye open. I was afraid of waking up in a white room.

I decided to write May's story to help me make peace with my own, as a kind of therapy. I needed to know that someone else had been there too. Though we were locked up a century apart, by sinking into May's story, I came back to life.

Marie has just broken off her engagement. She has no idea what she wants to do with her life. Her parents feel guilty for having pushed her towards marriage, and ask her to sit down with them one evening. Her father speaks first.

'I was wrong, I should have encouraged you to carry on with your studies. Today we're going to make a new start, we're going to follow our dreams. I've been teaching for over twenty years … that's long enough. I want to be a journalist, write for a living, have my own newspaper column. And I want to do it in Egypt. Cairo is the place to be right now. I've already published a few pieces in magazines over there, and I have friends there who can help us set up our new life'.

Her father tells her all about Cairo, how vibrant its newspapers, schools and universities are; he tells her about the generosity of Abbas II, the last Khedive of Egypt, who supported the independence movements. Back then Egypt was an oasis in the Arab world, a meeting place for intellectuals, writers and artists, people who wanted to awaken their nation.

Marie's parents give themselves a year to liquidate their assets and, in 1907, they all set off for Cairo.

On the bridge of the ferry, Marie looks out at the vastness of the sea, and thinks back on her childhood. She remembers the family home in Nazareth. She remembers Rih, the horse her uncle gave her, and the crazy rides they went on across the plains; Damascus and its souks that smell of leather and spice, her first oud, the Lebanese mountains, the sprawling gardens of her school in Aintoura, her broken engagement with her cousin, her brother's death …

A slew of questions amass in Marie's head and she makes the most of the long journey to put them to her father:

'I'm not sure I've completely understood everything. Why do you want to set up a university in Cairo, when there are already two in Beirut?'

'Cairo is a very special place. The cultural, political and social freedom there are like nothing else in the Arab world. But that's not the only reason. I also want you to be able to see for yourself the renaissance taking root in Egypt, and meet the people who are making it happen. There's nowhere else like it, and I want us to live there, where it's all happening, to be at the heart of it'.

After a fairly calm crossing, the Ziadeh family arrives at the port where two friends of Marie's father, Selim Chelfoun and Sheikh Ibrahim Hourani, are waiting for them. They greet each other affectionately, and then they all board the train bound for Cairo.

As soon as she sets foot in Cairo, Marie is swept away by its splendour. And the Nile is so beautiful: looking out on the river will be the only thing that can make her forget how much she misses the sea. As Marie walks through her new city for the first time, as she wanders its streets, crosses its bridges, admires its architecture, a strange yet familiar emotion takes hold of her. She feels as though she is rediscovering a world she has always known, a place that speaks to her soul. She feels in her bones that she will never leave this city.

Rooms have been reserved for them at the Savoy, in Soliman Pasha Square.

'Who was Soliman Pasha?' she asks her father, 'and what did he do to have had a square named after him?'

Marie's father smiles at her:

'Soliman Pasha didn't always go by that name. Before he moved to Egypt he was called Colonel Joseph Anthelme Sève. He was an officer in Napoleon's army, and he offered his services and military knowledge to Muhammad Ali the Great, the founder of modern Egypt. He converted to Islam, and took the name Soliman Pasha. He was the one that Muhammad Ali the Great entrusted to build up his army'.

The hotel is impressive with its sweeping entrance hall, its crystal chandeliers and its elegant gardens. At sunset they go down to dine on the terrace, where they are served by waiters in traditional costume. The food is exquisite. Around them, people are speaking different languages at every table. Exhausted from their journey, they return to their rooms. The night will be tender and calm.

The next morning, the Ziadeh family wakes early, They want to see the apartment their friends have found for them straight away. It's not far, so they'll go on foot. As she walks out of the hotel, Marie looks at the statue standing in the middle of the square.

'Is that Soliman Pasha?'

'Yes, my dear', her father replies.

He looks at his friend:

'Lead on, my dear Selim'.

They go down Qasr El Nil Street, a long and beautiful avenue lined with shops and cafés bustling with life. Marie cannot stop staring at everything going on around her, in awe of how animated her new hometown is. The apartment is close by, at 14 Mazloum Street.

As soon as they step through the door, Elias sees a smile of relief spread across his daughter's face. The rooms all lead off a large living area, which is separated from the bedrooms by detachable partition walls. If all the partitions are moved aside, the apartment becomes one big room in which the family will be able to host a large number of guests. Marie looks at her father and whispers in his ear: 'This apartment will be a great meeting place: think of the parties we'll be able to have'. Their complicity intrigues Nazha, Marie's mother. She is curious, and would like to ask her husband what Marie said. But Elias doesn't give her the chance, as he ushers the little group around the apartment. Adjacent to the living room, Marie discovers a small, peaceful room. She exclaims excitedly to her parents:

'This will be the music room, we can put the gramophone in here, and our instruments!'

Her parents are delighted to see her so happy, and they have fallen in love with the apartment too. So Elias begins his negotiations with the landlord. An hour later, it's settled. The landlord goes off to draw up the contract, while the Ziadeh family goes back to the hotel to pick up their things and bring them back to their new home.

The dream is just beginning.

The following days are spent settling in. Nazha decorates the apartment in the Eastern way, covering the walls with pictures and installing an enormous bookcase in the living room. Marie takes immense pleasure in setting up her music room. She puts her piano in there, as well as the oud and all the other instruments. In these halcyon days, the three of them go out to museums, the theatre, the opera. Wherever they go, Marie is struck by the diversity of cultures, languages and people.

Elias is their impromptu tour guide, he tells them that Khedive Ismaïl wanted to turn Cairo into a large and beautiful capital city, like Paris. He takes them to the Azbakeya gardens, a magical place overflowing with cafés, casinos and theatres. In the evening, the Ziadeh family dine together. Marie's mother has found a young Sudanese man to help her run the household. Bachir is very tall and very handsome, with dark skin and fine features. Often after dinner they all end up in the music room and spend the evening singing together.

It's 1907, and Mustafa Kamil launches a fundraising campaign to set up the University of Egypt. For Marie this is wonderful news, as she dreams of studying at a university.

On 21st December 1908, Mustafa Kamil's dream, and the dream of so many Egyptians, comes true. In the presence of Abbas II, the University of Egypt is officially declared open.

May's father's friends, Selim and Ibrahim, tell him that he can write for the newspaper *al-Mouktataff*, while he's waiting to find a more permanent job as a journalist – which they don't think will take him long.

While Elias is frequenting Cairo's intellectuals, Marie takes classes in Latin, Maths, English, French, Russian, German and Italian. She also works hard to bring her Arabic up to scratch; she already knows that this is the language she will choose to write her first texts in.

One day, a journalist friend of the family introduces them to Idris Ragheb, an obscenely wealthy aristocrat and owner of the newspaper *al-Mahrousa*, one of the names given to the city of Cairo and which means 'the protected one'. He is also President of the Masonic High Council of Egypt, a well-known man and a respected one. In a short space of time, Marie has managed to make a name for herself in the high society of Cairo. He asks her to give private lessons to his daughters.

Marie immediately warms to Fatna, Atiya and Amina, and the lessons begin the following day. Their classes become an oasis of joy, learning and discussion for the girls and for Marie. Ragheb's six sons quickly become jealous and ask if Marie can give them lessons too. But she is still ill at ease with men, and politely declines their request.

On 23rd April 1908, Marie arrives at Ragheb's house in mourning clothes. She cannot stop her tears from falling: Qasim Amin, the writer, militant and pioneer of feminism in the Middle East, has just died.

Even if she never met him, this exceptional man has been guiding her thoughts and her reading for a long time. She decides to spend the entire day studying his work with Ragheb's daughters. She tells her young charges about the modernity of his texts, his fight for the emancipation of women and against the wearing of the veil, against polygamy and against the practice of repudiation. She hammers into them the belief that became his manifesto: education is the path to freedom.

A few weeks later, Idris Ragheb asks her how she would like to be paid for these classes that she has been giving for nearly a year now. She replies that he must never talk to her of money, because the lessons give her so much pleasure. Besides, Ragheb's daughters introduce Marie to all of Egyptian high society, and Ragheb does the same for her father, and this is in itself a kind of payment. But Ragheb does not take no for an answer and hatches a plan that will turn out to be life-changing for the Ziadeh family. Not long after this, he invites them all to lunch at his house. After the meal, while they are enjoying their coffee, he announces: 'I'm giving you my newspaper, *al-Mahrousa*'. Marie cannot believe her ears. She looks incredulously at her father and at Ragheb.

The next morning, Nazha wakes up her daughter and her husband, and they go to an early morning meeting with Idris Ragheb at the *al-Mahrousa* offices, to sign the contracts and the transfer of rights.

Elias has decided that they will celebrate this extraordinary day by having a breakfast feast in the Shepherd, a large hotel that is Marie's favourite place to go. Situated right in the heart of Cairo, in the al-Ataba al-Khadra district, the Shepherd is frequented by the aristocracy of Cairo, European travellers, politicians and several journalists. Marie loves its atmosphere, its large rooms and its décor:

'Today will be a good day', she says, full of enthusiasm.

Elias Ziadeh has even arranged for a carriage ride along the banks of the Nile. And to celebrate the newspaper changing hands, he invites his future editorial team to eat at one of the best restaurants in Cairo, the St James, known for its seafood platters and exquisite fish. Ibrahim will be the chief editor, and Selim the main reporter.

On 11th January 1909 the first issue of the new *al-Mahrousa* is released.

Marie's days pass by at a heady pace: she gives her private classes, visits the newspaper headquarters and makes new acquaintances. Her command of Arabic is getting better every day. Encouraged by her father's friends, she sends her writing to Antoine Gemayel, writer and journalist at *al-Ahram*, and to Khalil Moutran, one of the greatest poets of the time. Both of them see the potential for greatness in her writing. She enjoys connecting with these Lebanese writers; it reminds her that despite her love for Egypt, sometimes she misses her homeland.

Like many Arab authors, Marie writes under a pseudonym. In *al-Mahrousa* and in other newspapers, she signs her work sometimes as Khaled Raafat, and sometimes as Aïda. Her first volume of poetry, written in French, is published in March 1911. This time, she publishes under the name Isis Copia, as an homage to the Egyptian goddess. The volume is titled *Flowers of Dreams* and is dedicated to Lamartine. It comprises forty-three poems and three narrative texts, including memoirs and a kind of private diary in French and in English. Bowled over by the talent Marie shows at such a young age, Khalil Moutran writes an effusive article in his newspaper and predicts that a great author has been born.

Not long after the publication of her book, Marie attends a conference organised by an activist group that fights for women's rights. The keynote speaker, Labiba Hashim, speaks about emancipation and the right to education. It suddenly dawns on Marie that not all women have the same opportunities she has. She leaves the hall with a single idea in her head: she wants to write an article about Labiba, explaining the reason behind her campaigning. Marie works all night long, spurred on by her subject matter. When the first rays of sunlight chase away the darkness, she puts the final full stop on her text and goes out onto the balcony to watch dawn break.

One day, Marie loses her watch, which is very precious to her. She looks for it everywhere: at home, at the office, everywhere, but it is nowhere to be found. This loss plunges her into a deep sorrow. So Marie decides to write an article in *al-Mahrousa* to explain how deeply it has affected her. A few days later, as if by some miracle, Bahithat al-Badiya writes directly to her in the pages of the newspaper:

'I have found your watch. I have it here with me and I'm taking good care of it. I understand how sad you were to have lost it. But, dear Marie, dry your precious tears. Come and see me instead. Your watch is waiting for you at my house ... it really is a special watch, it must have understood how much I wanted to meet you. In finding it again, you have also found a friend, a friend who has heard your voice in the articles you have written, who has understood the importance of your words. A friend who will be loyal to you'.

Bahithat al-Badiya is in fact the pen name of Malak Hifni Nasif, who at this time is writing a new series of articles in *al-Mahrousa* entitled 'Women'. Marie admires her greatly, but is far too shy to dare approach her. This is why she cannot believe her eyes when she reads Malak's invitation to go to see her at her home. Walking on air and very nervous, that very day she takes the train to Helwan, the village where Bahithat al-Badiya lives. Her heart is pounding in her chest, and she repeats to herself over and over again: 'Thank you! Thank you my dear watch!'

She arrives at nightfall in front of a villa built in the European style. The sky is lit up. Malak welcomes her with open arms, as if they were old friends. The two women settle down in a large living room painted red, amber and green. The conversation quickly turns to their favourite subject. For two hours, they talk of nothing but women, their position, their role in public life, the wearing of the veil, education for girls, the right to work ...

Marie tells Malak about her life in Cairo: the apartment, the private classes, the newspaper, her writing. Malak in turn wants to know how much progress the fight for women's rights has made in the Egyptian capital. She is a passionate and fascinating woman, with great energy. She has a compelling personality, she is intelligent and she dares to broach taboo subjects such as polygamy and repudiation. Throughout the whole evening, the spirit of Qasim Amin drifts over the conversation; his words and his thoughts reverberate in the room.

This first meeting will not be the last, and the two women say their goodbyes knowing that a common cause has bound them together for life.

A few weeks later, Marie starts translating a German book, *Deutsche Liebe* by Friedrich Max Müller. For as much as she finds this new challenge fulfilling, she is acutely aware that if she wants to make her mark in the cultural life of Cairo and of the Arab world, she needs a different name, one that does not have the religious connotations of Marie.

Tired of writing under a pseudonym, she requests a formal discussion with her parents. She had been terrified about how they would react, but is relieved to discover that they agree with her. They spend a good part of the evening debating what her new name should be. Every time her father suggests one, she rejects it, saying that it doesn't 'feel right'.

Then suddenly her mother gets up, disappears for a moment, and comes back with a book that she places in Marie's lap.

'When I was a child', she says, 'our class put on a play based on this book, *May and the Leaves of Autumn and Spring*, written by an English poet. I played the main character, May. I wished my name were May, but it came too late for me. When you were born, I so badly wanted to give you the name May, but I didn't dare say so'.

It's night. Alone in her room, Marie looks up the meaning of this name: May ... it is a name for fairies in Arabic poetry, it comes from ancient Persian and it means 'wine'. Poets still use it in that sense. Marie is overjoyed: she has finally found a name that feels right. And best of all, May could easily be taken for a diminutive of Marie, and so she is not abandoning her old self entirely.

May Ziadeh is born.

While the euphoria of May's new identity engulfs them, the heat of summer takes the Ziadeh family by surprise. Realising that the months to come will be suffocating in Cairo, the family decides to go to Dhour El Choueir on Mount Lebanon for a while. They make plans with old friends there, and the friends arrange everything perfectly for their arrival: the house is delightful, built from stone, with red tiles on the roof and a beautiful garden. Inside there are vaults and arches. From the first-floor balcony there is a splendid view over the valley.

May and her parents are overjoyed to see their friends from Lebanon. Everyone is so proud of May, whose career they have been following from afar. They loved her first collection, *Flowers of Dreams*, and they are looking forward to reading what May publishes next.

One day, they organise a surprise for her. While she is out on a walk, they ask her to close her eyes and let them guide her. They walk her along for a few minutes. When she finally opens her eyes, she is standing in front of a lovely little cabin. 'This will be your writing studio', they tell her. At the entrance, there is a board that says 'The Green Cabin'. May is lost for words ... and to top off this glorious day, they have prepared a delicious barbecue.

The very next day, May goes to her new sanctuary where she will henceforth spend most of her time reading and writing.

May has quickly established herself as a key player in the cultural life of Dhour El Choueir. At her friends' request, she agrees to give a speech and chair a debate at the village club, where she will talk about her volume of poetry and her next project. When the day arrives, she sees that the room is full to bursting. Choked by fear, terrified at the idea of talking in front of an audience, May looks down at her notes ... but she won't need them. Before long, the words are flowing by themselves. As she speaks, her father watches her, his eyes brimming with love and pride. Beside him, her mother cannot hold back her tears.

To celebrate the occasion, a sumptuous dinner has been prepared. In the course of the evening, May shares her enthusiasm for the book she has just finished reading: *Ar-Rihaniyat*, the latest book by Ameen Rihani, a Lebanese author living in the United States.

Georges, the president of the village club, tells her that he would like to organise a special meeting with the author for her. Seeing May's amazement, he says, laughing,

'Didn't you know that Ameen is from these parts? His village, Freike, isn't far from here. With your permission, I'll send him a message to ask if you can meet him'.

Rihani's response comes back quickly: he is delighted at the prospect of meeting the author of *Flowers of Dreams*. May is overjoyed. She is barely twenty-five years old and life is smiling on her. A few days later, she is on her way to Freike.

Anxious at the thought of meeting such an important person, May feels uncomfortable in her white dress and her flower-trimmed bonnet. She hangs back on the doorstep. But Rihani quickly puts her at ease: he is welcoming, smiling and warm. He answers all her questions patiently and generously. Rihani senses that a brilliant future awaits May. Deep within himself, he promises to be there for her and to watch over her.

After lunch, while all the other guests are resting, Rihani and May go out to walk around the village. May desperately wants to know whether he has a special place, a place that inspires him. Rihani decides to let her in on his secret, and takes her to his favourite spot. Their conversation focuses on writing and the creative process. They talk together until late in the evening, and this day marks the beginning of a long and beautiful friendship.

A few months later, another event changes the course of May's life. She discovers *Broken Wings*, the new book by Gibran Khalil

Gibran, a Lebanese writer also living in exile in the United States, and whose work she has followed closely for the past year. Bowled over by this story of an impossible love, May decides to write to the author to tell him how much she admires his work. Barely a week has passed before she receives a reply. She tears open the envelope and, trembling with joy, finds inside a letter several pages long. Gibran is grateful that she wrote to him and for the kind sentiments she expressed about his work. After several compliments and comments on her letter, he settles into a less formal mode. Gibran writes of Lebanon, of its mountains and of Bsharri, the village where he was born. His sentences are imbued with enormous nostalgia. When she has finished reading the letter, May is very moved, and replies to him immediately. Though she is usually so shy with men, she finds herself newly emboldened. She opens up to him too, telling him about her childhood, her family, her broken engagement, her reluctance to accept the rules imposed on women by society.

After several months of correspondence, each blue envelope strengthens the bonds between May and Gibran. Beyond the many points they have in common (their home country, their decision to live elsewhere, a love of music), they discover that they are passionate about the same books, that they share a thirst for knowledge and a love of writing.

Gibran is not the only one to write to her almost weekly. The young girl's friendship with Malak continues to blossom through an exchange of letters, and May takes great pleasure in asking advice from the woman she considers to be her role model.

In April, the University of Cairo organises a gala ceremony in honour of Khalil Moutran. The event is announced in *al-Mahrousa*:

'A gala is to be held in honour of Khalil Moutran, one of the greatest poets of our time. The ceremony will take place on 24th April at the University of Cairo'.

Gibran, who cannot leave American soil, sends a speech to May and asks her to read it aloud at the dinner. May wants more than anything to make Gibran happy, but her throat tightens at the thought of speaking in front of such an enormous group of people. Her parents reassure her, cajole her, remind her of the speech she gave in Lebanon the previous summer. Eventually she gives in. In addition to Gibran's text, she prepares a few words of her own in honour of her friend Moutran.

On the day of the ceremony, May is so nervous that she turns up two hours before the ceremony is due to begin. From backstage, she watches the room slowly fill with people. Every time she spies a literary personality her heart leaps, and she cannot tell whether it is from fear or excitement. Taha Hussein, a young blind journalist who campaigns against the traditionalists of al-Azhar, is also there. His reputation precedes him: he is known as 'the intellectual rebel'. His statements and positions are violent, but he always expresses them with great calm. May admires him enormously.

Before getting up on the stage, May thinks of Gibran. She wonders if he realises that it is because of him that she is about to do the bravest thing she has ever done.

She hears the speaker announce 'Miss May Ziadeh'. Her legs can barely hold her up, she is shaking and hopes no one will notice. Thankfully, because of the light of the projectors, she can't see the crowd sitting in front of her.

And so she begins to read, or rather to recite Gibran's words. She knows them by heart from having read and reread them so many times. Her voice is calm and measured. Little by little, the magic starts to take hold and her anxiety fades completely. Just like in Dhour El Choueir, the words flow spontaneously from her lips. The thunder of applause that breaks out when she reaches the end stops her from moving straight onto her own text. Then when she reaches the end of her speech, loud cries of 'Bravo!' resound in the room. People are getting to their feet to give her an ovation. May feels herself buckle.

After the ceremony, before she can even go out into the room, a crowd of men and women rush up to greet her and congratulate her.

When she returns home, May thinks about her future. Will she go to university, as she had planned? She had felt so at home amidst all those intellectuals ... She would like such events to happen more often. The idea hits her that she could offer a space where great minds could meet and exchange ideas. One of her friends, Lutfi El Sayed, tries to convince her that she should continue with her studies. Like May's parents, El Sayed believes that knowledge is the only path to freedom and emancipation. It is 1913, Europe is on the brink of war. May knows nothing of it and has not the slightest suspicion of what is to come. Her life is sheltered and all doors are open for her. In the end, she refuses to choose between her two preferred paths: she will open a literary salon and also enrol at university.

And so it comes to pass that every Tuesday evening the house is taken over by a joyful crowd of authors, poets, journalists and professors. In a short space of time, the salon has become the most important meeting place in the whole of Cairo society, to the point that Tuesdays have become known as 'May's day'. Idris Ragheb often comes by with his daughters, which makes May very happy. The whole Ragheb family is happy and proud to have contributed to her success. May is an attentive host, she serves her guests tea, coffee, sparkling rosewater and pastries. Her wit and her wisdom shine. She is often the only woman there, and is aware of her privileged position, vowing that her behaviour will be irreproachable in every way: 'I will prove that a woman can exist in this man's world, and I will do it for all those women who are less fortunate than me'.

At the same time, she has enrolled at the University of Cairo. She takes classes in Philosophy, History, Science and Ethics, and she loves her studies. She is often the first to arrive in the morning and the last to leave in the evening. As with everything she sets her mind to, she devotes herself to her studies with great application and energy.

Gibran's letters continue to arrive regularly. May is becoming more and more attached to this man whose spirit accompanies her everywhere. One day, he sends a portrait of her drawn in charcoal. When she discovers the gift, she is overcome with emotion ... their missives have become increasingly tender, and when they speak of the love of music they share, the poet writes to her: *'every time you play music, I am there, by your side. Didn't you feel my hand in yours right from the very first notes, the last time you picked up your oud?'*

A short while later, Bachir gets married. His wife is from the Siid region, in the south of Egypt. Nazha had employed her to help look after the running of the household. But Elias realises that the apartment is getting to be a bit small for two families, and decides to move. They set up the new place just like the old one. The main room is bigger, and the music room just as beautiful. Bachir has separate rooms apart from the family, and moves in there with his new wife. There is, however, one disadvantage. The apartment is on the fifth floor and the building has no lift. May feels embarrassed for her Tuesday friends. Some of them are very elderly and Yacoub Sarrouf in particular sometimes has difficulty getting around. But nothing will stop this iron-willed man who calls May 'my dear empress'. Every Tuesday, he climbs the five flights of stairs to attend her salon.

In August 1914, war breaks out. Some Arab countries are convinced that if they become allies of the French and the British, they will finally be able to overthrow the Ottoman Empire. But in Egypt, the people rise up against the idea of an alliance with the British. The government is mistrustful and demands concrete promises. At May's salon, the conversation shifts from literature and philosophy to geopolitics. In December, the British depose Abbas II and appoint his uncle Hussein Kamel in his place. They want Egypt to remain neutral rather than join forces with the Ottoman Empire. To set out his independence from Constantinople, Hussein Kamal takes the title of First Sultan. But this independence is only relative, as Britain officially places Egypt under protectorate. The Egyptians do not take kindly to this intervention. In the streets, the cries are heard all over: *Allah Haye! Abbas Gaye!* 'God lives, Abbas will return!'

II

When the First World War came to an end, it left a devastated world in its wake. Cairo entered a new era of fighting, doubts and sorrows.

Al-Mahrousa kept closing and reopening, because of censorship and the political positions it took, which were clearly and overtly pro-revolutionary. It was at this time that Taha Hussein, the blind journalist, came back from France, having finished his studies. He had married a Frenchwoman, Suzanne, whom he brought with him as soon as he started frequenting the Tuesday salon again. May saw her only very occasionally after their first meeting, whereas Taha was from that moment on one of her closest friends, the ones she would ask to stay on after the rest of her guests had left.

But the thing that most affected May during that period was the change in tone of Gibran's letters. At the beginning he had addressed her as 'dear great author', and then suddenly switched to 'my dear Miss May'. There was also a card that Gibran had had sent to her inviting her to the opening of his exhibition in New York, in a very well-known gallery.

She had sent a letter in response to his invitation, explaining her sadness at not having been able to share that moment with him. His reply took her by surprise:

'My dear May, I know that you are the only one who can awaken those who slumber. Do it, modernise their thinking through your writing, you can be a catalyst for them. In one of your letters you told me how happy you were to celebrate with me at al-Azbakeya after your speech at the university, and yet you still tell me now that you are sad not to have been able to come to the opening of my exhibition in New York!

Don't you remember?

II

We wandered, hand in hand, from one canvas to the next, and we stopped in front of each one to discuss it and analyse it, don't you remember that either?

It is dawn, I must take my leave.

I thought I had finished writing my letter to you, but then I opened the window and I saw snow, and suddenly I was a child again, in our Lebanon, our mountains. I can see the little snowman I've just made, May. I'm going out to walk in the snow, but I shan't be alone, you'll be by my side my dear May'.

That day, after she had given her speech, May had been paralysed by fear and had not managed to tell him what she was feeling. Gibran had taken it badly and had stopped writing to her for ten months. He only resumed their correspondence after she had written him a long and tender letter in which she asked for news of him. He wrote back:

'What can I say about my stupid silence in response to your letter, and that enduring smile of yours that lights up my existence ...'.

May published her book on Bahithat al-Badiya, a book in which she wrote the story of al-Badiya the woman, writer and militant. In it she explained and defended Bahithat's ideas, while also writing about the friendship they shared. She sent a copy of the book to Gibran, along with a letter. He was proud to see that their relationship and their discussions had pushed both of them to bring to fruition the ideas they developed together, and all the more so because he admired the result so much. Their correspondence resumed its former rhythm.

But how could she explain to him how afraid she was of love? She was afraid even of the word itself. She felt that what he was offering her was a kind of blackmail: love or nothing. He responded that she was being unfair and that it wasn't true that he wanted all or nothing, that he couldn't even see her, be with her in Cairo, that he had nothing to give but his words.

Although May was overjoyed by their closeness, she was well aware of where they diverged. For her, love found its ultimate fulfilment in marriage, which she considered a consecration of love. For him, marriage was destructive: he would say that 'marriage transforms men into slaves. If a man wants to liberate himself, he should divorce his wife and live as free as the air'.

But Gibran apologised for having pushed their relationship too far towards passion, and assured her that he did not want to rush her.

However, May's heart was already set on its path, the path of true love. A love above all else, love of the spirit and the soul. And Gibran started to call her 'my princess'. One day he wrote to her:

> *'My princess, this is the first time in five weeks that I've been able to write to you, because I have been unwell. My first words are for you'.*

To ease his suffering, May sent him a long letter and enclosed a photograph of herself, something that Gibran had been awaiting impatiently for a long time.

> *'Years ago, on the first Tuesday of my literary salon, I had this photo taken. I wanted to send it to you, but at the last minute I decided not to and I sent you the letter without this photo, which was always meant for you. Now it's yours, I am sending it to you. Better late than never'.*

The country was going through a difficult time; the British did not want to have any dealings with Saad Zaghloul. The revolution started up again, with greater momentum than before, but the leaders and politicians of the country refused to form a new government. Then the British arrested Zaghloul and exiled him again, along with some of his cronies, on one of the Seychelles in the Indian Ocean.

May wrote in *al-Mahrousa* about the unrest that was rumbling in the city. The streets were full of demonstrators, with their flags and their chants of 'Long live a free and independent Egypt!' and 'Long live Egypt, long live the fatherland!'

The Orient was finally awakening. The citizens were occupying the main square and rallying around a single goal: freedom and independence.

The next day, May marched with the crowd that was burying those who had fallen in the demonstration the day before. And that same evening she wrote: 'I saw in the people's faces the same strength and determination as yesterday; the same cries rang out. But today they were marching behind coffins crying out "Long live Egypt, long live the martyrs of freedom!" This word, chanted over and over by the crowds of people, echoed in the streets, the squares and all corners of the country, and would keep on ringing out: "Freedom!"'

Meanwhile, Huda Shaarawi had not faltered in her intense struggle alongside her female comrades. May supported them by defending their cause in the press and in her books. The situation in Egypt was slowly changing. In February, after Zaghloul's exile, there was a declaration that annulled the Protectorate of Egypt, and Sultan Fuad became king, the first king of Egypt. He got married for the second time in the middle of the revolution and took as his wife the woman who before long people would call Queen Nazli. As chance would have it, this woman, Nazli Sabri, was the granddaughter of Soliman Pasha.

In March 1922, the king declared Egypt's independence. In April, along with the new government he formed a committee to write the Constitution. Neither the Wafd Party nor the National Party was represented on this committee. That same month, the king passed the throne on to his son.

In the course of the next two years, many of May's friends wanted to come to Egypt to see what was going on. And so it was that Ameen Rihani surprised her by turning up at her Tuesday salon. It was an emotional reunion and they spent many special days together. May took him to see all the places she loved, the theatres and the cafés of Cairo. They each talked endlessly about their lives, and all they had been through in the long time that had passed since they had last seen one another. They arranged to meet up during the next summer break in Rihani's village, Freike, in the Lebanese mountains.

The Ziadeh family was exhausted from these years of unrest, from working so much and from the constant quarrelling between May and her mother, and so they had decided to spend the next summer travelling in Europe. But all that still seemed very distant; it would be a long time until summer came. For now, they had to carry on working. May wrote many letters to Gibran. Neither of them could go any length of time without writing to the other. Gibran told her of the joy he felt each time he received a letter from her. How he would read and reread it, and spend the whole day with her, savouring her like a fine wine.

'My dear May, finally you are here, I can talk to you, to your heart, without words. May, you are the closest to my heart, come, come closer so I may kiss

your eyes. And have a wonderful holiday in Europe, I'm sure you're going to love it'.

May wished for only one thing: to meet Gibran. To see him, in the flesh, to take him in her arms and walk alongside him. But she was too afraid to tell him, and so instead she threw herself into her work.

The Tuesday salon continued to enliven Cairo society. Everyone wanted to come, and new faces were always popping up. One of the new ones this year was Mustafa Saadeq Al-Rafe'ie. May had come across him some time previously. He was famous for his love of classicism, and his defence of tradition. May wanted to get to know him better, and so she invited him to the Tuesday salon even though she knew that it would make sparks fly, because of the rivalry between him and Taha.

When Taha was still a student, he had openly criticised Al-Rafe'ie's work in articles published in *Weekly Politics* magazine. After he graduated, he had continued to write for the magazine, and Al-Rafe'ie had begun to attack him back. There was also a rivalry between Akkad and Al-Rafe'ie, but this was more of an intellectual war that sometimes turned very aggressive. A war between the conservative traditionalists, Al-Rafe'ie and his friends, and the progressive innovators, Taha, Akkad and their friends.

Right from the start of their friendship, rumours abounded about Taha and May. Everyone said that they were lovers. People gossiped about their supposed romantic encounters. It was true that the two of them often stayed on together after everyone else had left the salon, that they spent a long time talking, singing and listening to music ... She would read him books and poems in Arabic, which his wife, who did not speak the language, could not do. Taha never failed to tell her so. And perhaps, if there had been no Gibran and no Suzanne, the two of them might indeed have lived a beautiful love story together.

That Tuesday evening, when Al-Rafe'ie arrived at the salon, May went to great lengths to ensure that he would not feel excluded. She greeted him warmly and was very attentive to him, as she was with every new arrival. But Al-Rafe'ie misinterpreted her kindness and attention.

The evening ended in the music room and, as usual, Taha stayed behind after the others had gone home and asked May to sing 'Ya

Hanaina'. For Taha, these moments were magical. He felt happy in May's company. Before he left the apartment, he would always end up telling her that he was jealous of the relationship she had with Gibran.

In 1923, Gibran spent two weeks of rest and vacation in Boston. He sent regular letters to May, and postcards with pictures of the masterpieces in all the museums and exhibitions he went to. In each one of his letters he wrote: 'may God bless your beauty'. In return, May dared, albeit with extreme modesty, to confess her feelings for him. For the first time, she spoke to him of love. And he replied: 'This is the letter that brings us closer to the empire of the gods'.

'You say you are afraid of love?
Why, my little one? Love is light, it is dawn, it is Springtime.
Are you afraid of Springtime?
Do not be afraid my dear May, I am here'.

May set off for her regular break in Palestine, a place she loved dearly. Then she went to Rome, where she visited the Vatican and received an honour from Pope Pius XI himself. She didn't dare tell Gibran, but she was just a hair's breadth away from suggesting that he come and meet her in Europe. However, she was so afraid of his reaction that she decided against it, and never told anyone that it had ever occurred to her, not even Gibran himself.

Their relationship had settled into something more tranquil. May had sent Gibran a birthday card and he, delighted to know that she was still thinking of him, wrote back: enclosed with his letter was a picture of Leonardo da Vinci's Saint Anne, and another card that had a De Chavin painting on it, and on which he had written:

'When I was younger, I used to say that De Chavin was the greatest painter
after Delacroix and Carrière, but today, now that the years have passed, I
think rather that he is the greatest painter of the nineteenth century. I would
even say that he is to painters what Spinoza is to philosophers: he is the
Spinoza of painting'.

He had also enclosed a wallet as a gift. And this gave May reason to suspect that her mother sometimes went into her room to look through her things, because there was no other way that she could have found out about it; it had been a long time since May had told her anything about Gibran's letters. Every time it would end up with her mother bursting into tears, and cursing the day she had ever heard of this Gibran. And her father would say to May: 'your mother has become completely hysterical, it's impossible to talk to her any more'.

The correspondence between Gibran and May carried on throughout that year. She was very worried for him and his state of health, and he was also very worried for her. Her eyesight was suffering because she read and wrote so much, and worked without stopping. To cheer Gibran up, May told him that she had had her hair cut very short, because she wanted to feel totally free, even in her appearance, and she recounted the over-the-top reaction of her Italian hairdresser who had almost wept when he saw her hair on the floor, and how he kept saying he was inconsolable because of his role in this 'barbaric deed'.

May began a new column in *al-Mahrousa*, called 'Khaliat an-Nahl', in which she gave readers the opportunity to participate in debates by submitting questions that were of interest to them. And then May herself would respond. This column took up a lot of her time, but also gave her great pleasure. She felt as though she was in direct contact with her readers, that the discussions were more meaningful for it, and that they were exchanging views on all aspects of society.

But after all she had been through, May wanted to take a little distance and go on holiday. She decided to return to Italy, where she had been invited to attend a conference. She went to Alexandria to take the boat, which remained her favourite mode of transport. And it was there that she learned the terrible news. *Al-Mahrousa*'s problems with censorship had never completely gone away, but that day her father was arrested and thrown in prison.

She cancelled her journey immediately, and went back to Cairo to be close to Elias and to find a good lawyer.

Letters of support came flooding in from all sides. Everyone wanted to know whether Elias Ziadeh was alright. After the trial, during which he was vindicated by the judges, his liberation was on the front page of all the newspapers, and *al-Mahrousa* released a special issue. Letters of congratulations arrived from Beirut, from Rome, from Damascus. That evening, everyone was at the Ziadeh house to celebrate Elias's release. May's mother was weeping with joy having spent several days weeping with worry. She had been so afraid ...

II

Gibran was ill, and growing ever weaker. *'I like being an invalid. When I'm ill I can escape myself, I can forget myself'*, he wrote to May. She was very afraid for him and tried to convince him to come to Cairo, where she would organise a grand ceremony in his honour. Alas, his state of health would not allow him to make the journey. May resigned herself to the belief that the forces of the universe did not want them to meet. And so she sent him poems to console him and to make the distance between them a little more bearable.

It was 1929. The year had got off to a bad start. For May, family was something sacred and so she found it ludicrous that she had cousins and other family members in Cairo, right there, close at hand, and yet she never saw them. Her father did not speak to his brothers and she had never understood why. Every time she tried to broach the subject, he completely shut down. It was clear that relationships within the family had always been strained. When, in 1925, they had set off on holiday to Lebanon for the last time, and May had gone back to her father's village in Chahtoul, she had found her uncle and her cousins deeply unpleasant. Even so, she loved Lebanon and life in the village, and she had even hoped to have a house built there that would become her hideaway.

But a terrible tragedy was about to befall her.

May worked a lot, and you could see it in her face. But she cared little about her health. Everyone noticed her drawn features when she went with her friends to the Groppi café, a place not far from the new apartment they had recently moved into. The apartment was bigger and grander than the previous two, and it had a lift for the Tuesday evening regulars. May practically had her own quarters there, a large bedroom and an office with an alcove for her cats. This office had become her haven. She liked her independence and the company of her cats. In particular, there was a large balcony where she had set up a little garden of jasmine and forget-me-nots. She would spend long mornings tending her plants and talking to them. And then the apartment was only five minutes from the Groppi, the new spot where all the intellectuals of Cairo society met up. Each one of them had their own special, reserved table. But that evening, May could not join them there, because she was to go and have dinner with her parents in a casino on the banks of the Nile.

She was just getting ready to go out when she heard a loud banging from the hallway. Someone was hammering on the door.

Her father had been supposed to come home earlier to pick her up and go to the casino together, but he would never have knocked like that. Her mother ran for the door, May hot on her heels. It was her father's colleagues. They were carrying Elias's body in their arms. Her father had just had a heart attack. A cry burst out of May's throat, the cry of a dying animal. And after that, nothing. Silence.

III

Every time May thought she was starting to feel better, a new catastrophe befell her. Gibran, the love of her life, died in 1931, and her mother a year later. May sank into a deep depression and retreated into herself, refusing to see anyone.

Her cousins took advantage of her weakened state.

Her father's family claimed a share of the inheritance. May reeled from the injustice. It was as if all those battles she had fought alongside Huda Shaarawi had, in the end, been no more lasting than the wind. May's ordeal with her stolen inheritance made her realise that there was a long way to go to secure women's rights. She was not equal in the eyes of the law, and this made her vulnerable to attacks from her cousins in Cairo, Elias and Ignatius Ziadeh, and from their father Youssef who had stayed in Chahtoul. The same uncle who years before had put a stop to her plan of building a house in the village.

When her father died, May had inherited a share in an ancient family home and its agricultural land. Until his death, her father had shared ownership of these with his brothers. Since May was a woman and an only child, her male cousins had the right to demand a share in her inheritance, and they did so insistently and aggressively.

May had a bad feeling about it all. As well as the family land in Lebanon, she had also inherited *al-Mahrousa*, along with its immense library, as well as the printers, her parents' shares and their jewels. She knew instinctively that her cousins would do anything to get their hands on what was rightfully hers. They even sent people from Chahtoul to see her, to instruct her to pay a large sum of money that she supposedly owed them.

May did not trust them at all. She sensed that things were closing in on her, and so she decided to ask her friend Akkad for advice. He sent her his personal lawyer, apologising for not being able to come himself. May wanted to mount a legal case against her cousins, but after Akkad's lawyer had studied her file, he told her this would be unwise. In the end, Akkad advised her to settle the matter amicably. May could not believe her ears. He hadn't even deigned to come and see her in person to offer up this pearl of wisdom! He was suddenly very busy, he no longer had the time to come and see her, and meanwhile her cousins were making her life hell. She was afraid that they would end up sending someone to do her harm. They were capable of anything and the only advice that Akkad, her so-called friend, could give her was to settle the matter amicably ... as if that were possible! May felt betrayed. This was the same Akkad who had been her friend, and had professed to be madly in love with her! She could not get over it and cut off all contact with him, after sending back all the letters he had written to her.

In great distress, she decided to enlist the help of another family member: Joseph Ziadeh, who had now become a doctor. May had been in love with him in her teenage years. At the time, he had not felt strongly enough about her, and had decided to devote himself to his medical studies in France. In spite of the way things had ended between them, May was still very fond of Joseph. And in her time of need, she instinctively reached out to him to ask for help. She wrote him several letters explaining what was happening to her, and Joseph wrote back assuring her of his support. And so May decided to make a public announcement concerning her plans for her own will, and declared that after her death she would bequeath her library to the country. Her cousins had the gall to come to her home to reprimand her, telling her in no uncertain terms that she had no right to donate items of such value, or to take decisions on this subject alone, because they too had a say in her inheritance, and she could not dispose of it in any way without consulting them beforehand.

Bachir, the Sudanese man who had looked after the household, had stayed with May, even after her mother's death. Along with her three cats, he had become her only companion. But by this point Bachir's health was also deteriorating. He wanted to go back to his village to be close to his wife. He was sad to leave May but he had no choice. And so May said goodbye to the last familiar face she had left.

III

She would sit alone for hours, listless and melancholic. She thought she could hear around her the voices of all those she had loved, as if they were still close.

In September 1935, she wrote a text entitled 'My Will', in which she recounted what was happening to her.

> 'I am writing this letter today to make it known that after a thorough search, I have discovered that documents have disappeared from my home and from the newspaper offices. I have also been robbed of some jewellery. I should have had it all put in the bank, and I will do exactly that with the rest when I am feeling better.

> 'I love you, my Egypt, my Orient: I offer my life to you.

> 'I forbid anyone to try to make me leave my home, to sedate me, or to drug my food. I forbid anyone to touch my belongings, my documents and my letters, or to use them for any reason without my permission'.

Spiritualism, clairvoyance and mysticism became May's favourite pastimes. Her friends grew alarmed: she no longer took their calls, and the last time that a doctor had been to see her he had reported back to them that May was sinking into a deep depression, believed herself to be persecuted, was sad and alone. Her friends tried to tell her what was being said about her, and to cheer her up, but she refused to let them in.

May wondered to herself: 'What are they all getting so worked up about? Why on earth is it inappropriate to mourn for the people who were dear to me? I have lost my father, my true love and my mother. What more do they want from me? Yes, I'm unhappy. And? I have the right to be unhappy, don't I? So why can't they leave me in peace?'

One day, someone came knocking at her door and was so persistent that May – who hadn't answered the door to anyone in a long time – opened it a fraction. It was a young man who, taking her by surprise, pushed his way into the apartment. There he stood in front of her, not moving, just looking at her. May had lost a lot of weight, and her eyes were sore. She was pale, and considerably weakened by her illness. She was afraid he would not know who she was, so much had she changed. She was wearing a long, loose-fitting white *galabeya* that made her pallor even more pronounced. The apartment was plunged into half-darkness; a lone beam of light came from a little lamp set beside an ashtray full of cigarette butts, in which a cigarette was still burning away.

May stood there in front of the young man, watching him without saying a word or moving a muscle. She did not even invite him to take a seat. She just looked at him, with a strange kind of smile. As if she were begging him, silently, to leave her alone with her memories.

Eventually the young man broke the silence:

'I'm speaking on behalf of everyone who loves and respects you. I beg you, let us be here for you, let us help you find your way out of this solitude. Do not despair, do not give up; you must fight. You must rediscover your zest for life. Let me bring a little joy to your life. Let me stay by your side'.

May stood there, facing him, watching him. She was overcome by a feeling of tenderness, and moved to tears. In a weak voice, barely audible, she replied:

'Thank you, thank you … there's nothing, nothing. I don't need anything, I just want to sleep …'.

He took one last look at her and left as suddenly as he had arrived.

May closed the door gently behind him.

Towards the end of the year, Joseph's wife died. He sent a letter to May to announce that he was coming to see her. Hope was returning!

For the first time in her life, May was no longer interested in what was happening beyond the walls of her home. She stayed on her own and did nothing, nothing but wait.

Finally Joseph arrived and knocked gently on the door of her apartment. May received him in her bedroom, she no longer had the strength to sit up in the living room. After she had offered her condolences for the death of his wife, she thanked him for having come to see her so swiftly, since she knew how much his children must need their father in this time of mourning. Joseph explained that he had come especially for her, and only for her, that he was there to help and protect her:

'I will not go back to Lebanon alone, I'm taking you home with me. You need a change of air, you need someone to take care of you, someone who will give you the attention and the love that you deserve. And that person is me'.

Joseph spent a month and a half in Cairo. He went to see May every day, and told her about everything he was doing for her. He had been advised to let a doctor examine May, and then to take her away somewhere peaceful for a while so that she could rest. Huda Shaarawi believed that what May was going through was perfectly normal, since losing loved ones is a terrible thing for anyone to endure. Huda gave Joseph the address of a sanitorium in Switzerland. She assured him that May would return in a much better state if only he could convince her to go. But Joseph did not share her view. After telling May about Huda's suggestion, he said to her:

'They don't understand that what you need is to come back to the pure mountain air and be with your family. I think you should come back to Lebanon with me, that would do you more good than all the clinics and luxury hotels in the world. What do you think, dear cousin?'

'I think you're right', she replied. 'I want to go back to Lebanon with you'.

It seemed to May that her cousin was a gift from heaven. He took care of everything: her day-to-day business, her documents, storing her things. He spoke to her gently. Once, he asked her to sign a power of attorney that would let him look after everything that belonged to her, so that he could keep an eye on it all and she could finally find some peace. She replied that she had nothing in Egypt, that all her affairs were managed by third parties, that she didn't need to do anything and that his help was not necessary. Even so, he stood his ground and asked her to think about it some more.

The next day, he returned with two men May had never seen, and introduced them as his relatives. They stayed close beside Joseph throughout their visit, and for the remainder of his time in Cairo. These men had appeared out of nowhere and didn't leave his side for a moment. One day, they came with two other men who worked as clerks at Abdeen Palace, the government headquarters.

One of the men opened a big book on May's bed, and asked her to sign it. One of Joseph's relatives produced a pen, and May looked at her cousin.

Joseph said to her: 'It's to sort things out to get your passport processed easily'.

No one will ever know what went through her head in that moment. Even though she had refused to grant her cousin power of attorney, May smiled at him to indicate her consent. She looked up to ask the clerk where she should sign. The clerk looked at her intently, then showed her the two places where she was to sign. She signed May Ziadeh and, beneath it, Marie Ziadeh.

At the beginning of March everything was ready: May had her Egyptian passport in her hand, and her suitcases were packed. The house was tidy, the furniture covered, everything was ready for her departure. And yet May was overcome by doubt: she no longer wanted to leave Cairo, or her apartment. Joseph had sworn to her on his children's lives that the house in Cairo would remain untouched, and that he would bring her back to Egypt whenever she wanted, even if it was the day after she arrived in Beirut.

IV

The day they left, May's face was radiant. She took the train from Cairo with Joseph, and when they drew closer to Lebanon she wept. After all she had been through, she was back in the land of her birth, her beloved Palestine. It was the greatest joy she could imagine.

On the Lebanese border, at Naqoura, the border police and the customs officials recognised her and welcomed her with great ceremony, as if she were a film star. It made her feel very happy.

When they arrived in Beirut, Joseph welcomed her into his home, where he had prepared a room for her. The four of them were going to live there together, with the nanny who looked after his two sons.

After the first week, May began to feel ill at ease. She did not like being constantly surrounded by people she did not know well, nor feeling obliged to make an effort for them. And she was not used to living with children, and Joseph's boys were very noisy. At the beginning, she would receive her friends regardless, but very quickly she began to feel the need for her own space. She asked Joseph to set her up in a small apartment where she would feel at home, as he had promised her he would. May had never agreed to live with others, she needed to be on her own. She kept insisting that she wanted to live alone. But Joseph would not listen.

In great distress after two weeks of constantly making the same plea to Joseph and it falling on deaf ears, May shut herself up in her room and refused to speak to him. She could hear him on the other side of the door, speaking to the nanny in a loud voice as if he wanted her to hear what he was saying. He was saying all sorts of things. Once she even heard him say, 'Watch out, I think she's about to lose it. Don't let her near the children, and make sure they don't go near her. Don't try to go into her room, I'm worried she might harm the children'.

May was stunned, and almost opened the door to tell him what she thought of him, his children and the nanny. She could not believe her ears: her, harm Joseph's children! She did not understand why he would tell such lies, but she decided to keep quiet and stay shut up alone in her bedroom.

A short while after this, she asked him to let her return to Egypt. He had promised that he would let her leave straight away if that was what she wanted. She tried to rationalise with him: 'I'm asking you either to let me take an apartment of my own here, or to let me go back to Cairo'. But Joseph still refused to listen to her.

He introduced her to an Orientalist friend of his, an Englishman he had known for a long time and who had heard of May and wanted to meet her.

Mr Miller came to visit May several times, and they talked together about politics, poetry and English literature. But she lost patience very quickly; meeting with this man simply to please Joseph irritated her. She just wanted her cousin to let her leave. What's more, every time she wanted to access her money, she had to ask Joseph's permission. She didn't understand what was happening to her at all. She was consumed with misery and fear. She had already been there for two and a half months, and Joseph clearly had no intention of letting her have her freedom. And so one morning she decided to go on a hunger strike.

She knew now that she had made the biggest mistake of her life in asking Joseph to help her and in putting all her faith in him. How could she have done it? How could she have forgotten all the harm that he and his family had caused her? Why had she sent him that wretched letter? But all these questions were futile: May realised that she had fallen into a trap.

One morning, in the early hours, while she was still in bed, May awoke to the sound of someone trying to force the door of her room. The lock gave way and she saw the man she knew as Mr Miller burst into the room, accompanied by a doctor and a nurse.

She screamed. There was nothing she could do but scream.

The nurse looked at Miller and said, 'What shall we do, Doctor?'

In that moment, May realised with terror the trap they had set, and she screamed louder. The doctor nodded his head, and they jumped on her.

First they pinned her down, then they bound her in a straight-jacket, and finally injected her with intravenous morphine. May screamed with fear and pain: 'HELP!' She called for somebody, anybody, everybody; she even screamed to Joseph to help her.

Joseph did not reply, and there was no one else there to care.

May ended up on the back seat of a black car, with the doctor on one side and the nurse on the other.

Trapped in a straightjacket, drugged by morphine, she was driven through the streets of Beirut, tears flowing down her face. 'Oh my Beirut, how can you let me pass through you in this convoy of humiliation and pain? How can you stand by and watch the tears I shed in this car? Alone in this cruel world, I can see the fate that awaits me …'.

The black car drew up in a small courtyard, in front of a sinister-looking grey building. A nurse and some auxiliary nurses were waiting for her. They opened the back door of the car and tried to help her get out, but she refused their help and struggled out by herself, still in the straightjacket. She kicked the car door shut behind her. Everyone was watching her, standing there, in the middle of the courtyard, alone in front of all these people. Her expression was inscrutable, her head held high.

May shook her head, as if she were in the middle of a nightmare and this action would be enough to wake her up.

But it didn't happen. She was still there. She walked towards the entrance, ushered by a member of staff who was leading her to her new home: a psychiatric asylum.

In the corridors inside, she passed by a mirror, and stopped for a moment to look at her reflection.

It was the first time she had seen the state she was in. She barely recognised herself. 'Is that me? Is that really May? The elegant intellectual who always looked after herself and dressed well? Is that really what has become of me?'

There was nothing left of May.

They took her to a bedroom. The nurse who had been waiting at the entrance had been assigned to May. She came up to her and said: 'My name is Esther Wakim. If ever you need anything, all you have to do is call me or push the button beside you and I'll be right here for you'.

May turned her head away and said nothing.

*

It was 16th May 1936, two and a half months after May had arrived in Beirut.

She had decided to fight. The only weapon she had was resistance, and so she refused to talk or to eat. She kept reassuring herself: 'I just have to hold on until my friends in Cairo find out what's going on and come to help me. I just have to hold on a few days, time enough for the news to reach them. Taha, Lutfi, Moutran and Gemayel won't leave me here alone. They're my knights in shining armour. They'll come for me, I know they will'.

But the months passed and nothing happened.

Not a single friend, not a single person, not a soul came to see May. She received no letter, no word from anybody.

May stayed alone in her room watching the door, hoping it would open, that someone would finally come. In her head the questions rained down:

'What's going on? Where are they? Why is no one worried about my disappearance? Why have none of them tried to find out what has become of me? Why has no one come to my aid?'

The doctors trooped into her room day and night to try to convince her to eat and to talk. How could they think even for a second that she would agree to speak to them? They were Miller's accomplices, that same Miller who had lied to her and conspired with Joseph to trap her and lock her up.

May was impenetrable. Every time they came to see her, every time they tried to convince her to eat and to talk, she closed herself off even more. The doctors did not yet realise just how determined she was.

The only person May began to let close to her a little was Esther, the nurse. In the way Esther looked at her, in the way she touched her or came close to her, May could sense affection. She could also see how happy it made Esther to know that she was the only one to whom May showed any sign of life. She could see in the way Esther looked at her the gratitude she felt towards May for not lumping her in with the others. All the same, even though Esther too begged her to eat, May would not be persuaded.

The doctors threatened her, and said they would lock her in a cell if she carried on refusing to eat.

In the face of their threats, May did not waver.

She could feel herself dying slowly, and she was happy to know that she was so close to the end, to death, to freedom.

One morning, the doctors tried to force her to eat. A group of them burst into her room. Esther, her nurse, was there too, but the doctors had pushed her aside. She stood there, helpless, looking on with tears in her eyes. They forced May's mouth open. She screamed, she kicked them and hit out at them. Everything they stuffed in her mouth, she spat out instantly. She clamped her teeth together to form a barrier.

That was when the torture began. They had a machine brought in, a strange contraption covered in tubes.

They inserted the tubes into her nose, and pumped a liquid down them, a mixture of protein, eggs and milk. A few days later, they noticed that the tubes in May's nose weren't working; she kept pulling them out. They decided to insert the tubes down her throat instead. May wouldn't let them: she clamped her teeth shut and refused to open her mouth. So they broke her teeth. They smashed a hole in her front teeth, big enough to push the tubes through and then feed them down her throat.

May was just waiting to die.

One morning, she confided in Esther:

'I don't know whether a quick death, a sudden death, is an easy way to die. But I do know that a slow death, this death, pumping this food into my body through these tubes, is unbearable'.

When Joseph came to see her, May begged him to get her out of there. She described in detail what was being done to her and Joseph just smiled. He had got what he wanted: May's inheritance.

At night, she would force herself to vomit up whatever they had pumped into her during the day. They came to her room with a final threat: 'If you carry on behaving like this, we'll send you to the basement'.

Unaware of what that meant, May carried on with her hunger strike.

And so they followed through with their threat.

They sent her to the basement, and the cockroaches succeeded where all the doctors in the asylum had failed: May ate.

They had locked her in a dark room. There were no windows, and it was teeming with vermin. During her waking hours, May wept all the tears she had in her body. She kept screaming, 'HELP ME!'

The only reply she got was the noises made by Esther, who came every day to bring her food. May was no longer allowed any human contact, she was completely cut off. Isolated. Esther would put down the plate and then stay there, pressed up against the other side of the door. May could hear her sobbing. She knew that Esther came in the night to weep outside her door.

In the darkness of her cell, May would talk to her mother. 'Mama, come to me now, look at what they have done to your daughter. How can you bear what they have done to me? Mama, please, don't leave me alone with all these cockroaches ... Mama, I'd like to go and lie down on the grass, by a river, surrounded by flowers, near my home, in the mountains of Lebanon that overlook the valley. Oh mother, your daughter is being tortured, your daughter is dying of pain and grief'.

She spoke to Gibran too: 'Come to me, come and see the love of your life. I have become like your madman ...', and she would recite whole passages of *The Madman*. She called on Gibran to give her strength, and every time she spoke his name, a sigh of relief would gasp out from her soul. And Esther's sobs mingled with her own.

*

The doctors finally agreed to listen to Esther, who assured them that May had started eating again and that, if they allowed her go back to her room, she would do as she was told.

Esther helped May to get through it all. Sometimes, even though it was forbidden, they would talk to one another through the door. And so it was Esther who told her the good news:

'Soon you're going to be able to go back to your room. I told them you had agreed to eat normally. But if they take you back to your room, promise me you won't let them bring you here again'.

May promised, and was finally allowed to leave the darkness of the basement. A friendship had formed between her and Esther. No one would ever be able to understand May like Esther could, for she was the one who had witnessed May's misery and her humiliation.

May awaited Esther's arrival every day, sitting on the edge of her bed. When she saw Esther come in, she would hold out her hand and Esther would slip her a cigarette, even though it was strictly against the rules for the 'lunatics' to smoke.

Esther would leave her alone for a short while, and then come back to collect the little envelope in which May had hidden the cigarette butt and the ash.

May would say to her:

'Bury it in the ground, it's a mortal sin'.

Esther had become her confidante. May told Esther all about her past, her glory years, her sadness, and her feeling of having been betrayed by the people she had trusted.

'How is it that none of them have ever come for me? When I've been waiting for them all these months?' she said to Esther. 'They came to see me in Cairo after my parents died and after Gibran died. They said, "You'll come and travel with us, dear May. To Lebanon, your home, you will find happiness in your own country, and you have family there who will support and protect you!" And instead it was hell that awaited me here. In Lebanon I have been locked up, I have been humiliated, I have been tied up, put in a straightjacket and thrown into this asylum, Asfourieh, where death has closed in on me so many times'.

Esther told May that in the Egyptian newspapers it had been reported that she had fallen into a depression and had completely lost her mind, that she had gone mad and that her family in Lebanon had had her sectioned in a psychiatric hospital to make her well again.

How could her friends have believed this web of lies? Why hadn't they come, at least to see for themselves if it was true? What's more, some of them had become very powerful. Ministers, university chancellors, important men. And so why hadn't anyone done anything to stand up for her and to get her out of that hell, since she'd always been there for them, and now she had no one?

As she pondered it all and time went by, eventually she reached the conclusion that she would have to give up all hope of anyone coming to rescue her from that place. She was convinced that she would never get out of the asylum. She no longer expected anything from anybody; she ate her food and she took her medicine, as she had promised Esther she would. The violence towards her stopped; the psychiatrists even let her walk around the sprawling garden, with Esther by her side. There was a little bench that she liked to sit on, where she would look out over Beirut and the sea below. Esther carved the word 'May' onto their bench.

V

After seven months in the Asfourieh asylum, when May had lost all hope of ever seeing a familiar face again, the miracle happened.

The door to her room opened. May assumed it was Esther, as usual. And so she was astonished to see a different face, the face of Maroun Ghanem, one of Haifa's most prominent merchants, and an old friend of her parents.

May could not believe her eyes: her face lit up. For the first time in seven months, she smiled. Tears coursed down her face when she saw Maroun standing there beside Esther, who was smiling beatifically through her own tears.

May told Maroun everything, from the moment Joseph had come to see her in Cairo to the moment Maroun had opened the door of her room in Asfourieh. For two and a half hours, it all poured out of her. Maroun sat beside her, listening intently.

When she had finished, he told her that he had come to spend the winter holidays in Lebanon, his homeland, and that since it had been a while since she had last replied to any of the letters he had sent to her address in Cairo (Maroun was a great admirer of May's work, and closely followed everything she did), he had started to worry about her disappearance. And so he had made contact with the only member of her family that he knew in Lebanon, Dr Joseph Ziadeh. That was when Joseph had told him that May had gone mad and that for her own safety he had put her in the Asfourieh asylum. Otherwise, she would have ended up harming others, or herself.

Maroun said to her: 'To be honest, I didn't believe him'.

Finally, there was someone who hadn't believed this lie, finally someone who had heard her cries, her calls for help!

Maroun continued:

'I asked to see you, but Joseph did all he could to persuade me not to come. When he realised I wasn't going to give up so easily, he told me that you weren't allowed visitors. There was something suspicious about the whole thing, and so I decided I had to come and see you for myself. And here I am'.

Maroun asked her to promise him she would stay positive, to take care of herself and to eat. He asked Esther to help him nurture May's inner strength.

He looked her straight in the eyes and said: 'My dear May, my child, stay calm. We will get you out of here'.

He promised her that he would not return to Haifa until he knew she was safe, and out of that hell.

He spent months petitioning Dr Miller, and meeting with May's cousins. He even went as far as threatening to go after them himself if they refused his request. He visited May regularly, and brought her everything she needed. After persevering for months, Maroun finally managed to get her transferred from Asfourieh to a 'normal' hospital.

Three months of relentless effort just to get Joseph to concede a little.

May was taken to Rebeiz hospital on 23rd March 1937. She was weak and exhausted. Esther was by her side. Dr Nicolas Rebeiz, the director of the hospital, greeted her personally, with his assistant Dr Ghosn and another nurse who was assigned to take care of May during her stay there. The doctor introduced her to May, saying, 'This is Alice Salameh, your nurse'. May was taken to room 50.

Maroun was proud of May and of her courage: she had kept her promise. Maroun left Beirut a fortnight after her arrival at Rebeiz hospital. As he had promised her, he did not leave until he knew that she was out of danger.

Before he left, he had asked Alice, the nurse, to keep him updated regularly about May's well-being, and to contact him if ever she had cause for alarm. Only then did he go back to Haifa.

As soon as she arrived at Rebeiz hospital, May's health improved. Alice looked after her well, and May began to eat again. But since her teeth hurt her because of the brutal way the Asfourieh doctors had broken them, May did not allow Alice to remain in her room while she ate. She had to leave the tray and then go, closing the door behind her, if May was going to eat. Alice would wait on the other side of the door and keep watch to make sure that no one went in and took May by surprise while she ate. She did not want anyone to see the way she was now reduced to eating; it was far too humiliating for her.

In the afternoons, Alice would come and keep her company. She reminded May that they had met before, in 1925, while May was in Beirut at the Bassoul hotel. Alice had come to see her with Habuba Haddad, a journalist and author who held a literary salon in Beirut just like May's in Cairo. Her meeting with May had left a deep impression on her.

Alice was delighted to see May gain a little weight. May had noticed how distraught Alice had seemed when she saw her arrive at Rebeiz hospital, and now she understood why Alice had looked at her as she had: Alice had met her when she was beautiful, in her glory years, and now she had before her a weakened woman, thin, pale, hollow-eyed, with white hair and broken teeth.

The patient in room 51, just next door to May, was a woman from Damascus called Badiya Al-Ayoubi. She and May met and became friends, and Badiya introduced May to all the members of her family. Her father had been Prime Minister of Syria. Her aunts, the princesses Samia and Zahra Al-Jazairi, were the wives of princes Khaled and Mukhtar Al-Jazairi, the direct descendants of Emir Abdelkader Al-Jazairi. May started to feel less and less alone: she told her story to this distinguished family, and they adopted her immediately as one of their own. They already knew her in a way, because of her work. But they were appalled by what had happened to her and determined to do all they could to help her. May's circle of her friends, which had shrunk so drastically, started to grow again.

During May's convalescence, Joseph tried to see her several times. But she had asked Dr Rebeiz to forbid him access to her room. She refused to let him near her, and along with him all of those who had abandoned and forgotten her. She said to Esther, to Alice, to Badiya and her family that she would never be able to forgive them.

One day, Alice burst into May's room screaming with joy:

'Finally, someone has spoken out!' And she held out to May a copy of *al-Makchouf*. *Al-Makchouf* was a well-regarded newspaper in Lebanon, and its owner, Fouad Hbeich, had even set up a literary salon with the same name. It was Hbeich himself who had written the article about May, in which he told the story of all the injustices she had suffered.

V

May looked at the words written on the page, but she could barely make them out. Tears of joy filled her eyes: finally someone was standing up for her. It was 17th November 1937.

After the publication of that article, things moved very quickly. Other newspapers and journals picked up the story. In Cairo, too, news of May's ordeal was published everywhere. Hbeich and *al-Makchouf* had pushed hard, even going as far as to ask the Egyptian consulate to intervene and review the situation and, if necessary, to set up an investigating committee to get to the bottom of what had really happened. Hbeich and his colleagues set up a campaign to defend May and get justice for her. Arab authors the world over were up in arms about what was happening to her. The wind was finally blowing in her favour. People started to want to come to see her, but May felt like an animal in a zoo and did not want to see anybody, especially not any of the people who had abandoned her.

One day, the door to her room opened suddenly and Ameen Rihani burst in. May looked at him for a moment and then turned her head away. He persisted in talking to her anyway, telling her stories, and saying that he was going to do all he could to help her and get her out of there. May remained silent. Almost thirty minutes passed without her moving a muscle or uttering a word. Then Alice came back into her room and Rihani tried to enlist her help in convincing May to talk to him. His efforts were in vain: May refused to even look at him. Faced with this rejection, Rihani had no option but to leave the room. Before he left, he said:

'I'm not giving up, even if you don't want to talk to me. I will return, you'll see. This time, I'm here to stay'.

A few minutes later, her friend Badiya Al-Ayoubi came into her room and asked for her permission to let in Rihani, who was waiting on the other side of the door. But even Badiya did not manage to break May out of her silence, or even get her to so much as look at Rihani.

Three days passed, during which Rihani kept meeting with the friends who were now May's close circle: the Al-Jazairi family, the Ayoubi family, the Koury family and Fouad Hbeich, trying to get them to persuade May to agree to see him. After three days of arbitration, May finally agreed.

There stood Rihani, before May, in her hospital room. She looked him straight in the eyes and said to him:

'You stood by when they took me away from Cairo, you stood by when they threw me in the Asfourieh asylum, you stood by when I was in hell. Oh yes, Rihani, you did! You were there in my thoughts, I was furious, I raged against you. I couldn't stop wondering: "How is it possible that Rihani believes what they're saying about me, believes these lies about my so-called madness?" I swear to you, Ameen, I told myself that even if the whole world believed I was mad, you wouldn't believe it, you knew who I really was. I said to myself, "He'll never believe what they're saying about me, he'll come and save me". I was so sure of it, and I waited for you. That's why I'm so angry, I waited for you for so long and you never came'.

Rihani was silent for a few moments, and then he replied:

'I'm here now. I've come for the sake of our friendship. Forgive me, and tell me everything'.

Hours passed, during which she told him all about her ordeal in the most minute detail. The silence, the hunger strike, the solitude, the violence, the cockroaches, the feeding tubes in her nose, the broken teeth, all of it.

'There you go, now you know everything', she said. Rihani looked at her and replied:

'Get dressed. I'm taking you far away from this hospital'.

'And where can I go, Ameen? I have nowhere to go. I have no money, they took everything from me and put me under guardianship. Joseph has absolute power over me. Can you believe it, the only man I loved during my youth, and his brother, the only man I was ever engaged to, they're the ones who have waged this war on me. They had me tied up and they stole from me, they took everything from me. They inherited my fortune while I was still alive'.

The day after his visit to May, Ameen Rihani launched a huge media and legal campaign to get May out of this trap, to give her back her freedom and her rights. Thanks to him and his friends, things got better for May. Rihani began to do the rounds of all the guilty parties. The Egyptian consul was a friend of Joseph's, and was his main support. Rihani realised immediately what was going on, but even though Joseph had the help and backing of the consul, Rihani and May's friends did everything they could, with the help of Dr Rebeiz, to get May out of hospital and into an apartment that she could call home.

V

He had to convince Joseph to agree to this transfer, and specifically to pay the rent on the apartment that she would live in.

Once again, Rihani took it upon himself to thrash out a solution with Joseph. He had also discovered that Joseph had gone back to Cairo while May was in Asfourieh, and that he had emptied her apartment and sold the majority of her belongings, including all her books. And that he had put everything that remained in another small place that he had rented under his own name.

Joseph was wily and cunning. He kept making Rihani promises he did not keep. He just wanted to buy time: telling Rihani that he would agree to May being taken to a little apartment of her own, and that he was willing to pay for everything, and then disappearing. He kept claiming that he couldn't find a suitable place, and then that he wanted detailed assurance of how she would cope once she was alone in her new residence. Rihani came right back at him with the information that Esther, her nurse, would move in with her.

While they were waiting for the matter to be resolved, every time that Rihani came to visit May, they spent unforgettable moments together. They would talk about the past, the friends that had gone before them and the people they had loved. May was happy to have her friend Rihani back by her side again.

Joseph carried on refusing to sign her out of the hospital. He kept coming up with new excuses: he even had the gall to say that he wanted another medical opinion. May's friends, beside themselves with rage, called on Georges Khayat, an esteemed professor of psychiatry, who examined May and wrote up his report. Unsurprisingly, he approved the idea of transferring May to a private residence, with a nurse to look after her. Rihani presented the report to Joseph himself. But Joseph refused yet again, claiming that he was obliged to seek permission from the Egyptian consul. Rihani and his friends were aghast, but they continued to accommodate Joseph's absurd demands. The consul's attitude came as an even greater shock: he said that he could not give his approval for the transfer until he had the agreement of the Minister of Foreign Affairs in Egypt. Rihani left this meeting in a rage, and issued Joseph with an ultimatum:

'I'm giving you ten days. If the response from your friend the consul and the Minister of Foreign Affairs does not come back in May's favour, there will be an article about you in the news. I will

bring you down! Don't cross me Joseph, I've had enough of your games. Ten days, you have ten and not a day more.'
Rihani went back to the hospital and told Dr Rebeiz everything. Rebeiz decided to go and speak to Joseph himself. He left to go and meet with him, and came back astounded by the relentless determination of May's cousins to destroy her life.

He looked at her intently and said:
'May, get up and leave the hospital'.

All her friends were with her: the Al-Jazairis, the Ayoubis, the Khourys, and of course Esther. They gladly helped her to pack her suitcase. They didn't even think about where she would go; for the moment, all they wanted was to get her out of there. Just at the moment when everything was finally ready, Dr Ghosn, Dr Rebeiz's assistant, came in suddenly to announce that the Egyptian consul had just blocked the transfer, and that if the hospital staff let May go, they would all be held responsible. The only people who had the power to agree to the transfer were the cousins from Egypt and the Egyptian Minister of Foreign Affairs.

It was all too much. May's friends decided to take the case to court.

They approached two of the greatest lawyers of the time: Bahij Takeieddine and Habib Abu Shahla. The two men presented the case to the public prosecutor, with all the documents and reports from prestigious medical professionals such as Dr Rebeiz and Professor Khayat.

The prosecutor, Wajih Khoury, went to see May, after having met Joseph and heard what he had to say. After this, Khoury ordered that May be transferred from the hospital to a private residence.

But her ordeal was not over yet. May did not leave Rebeiz hospital until early January 1938, to go to the American hospital in Beirut, while waiting for an apartment of her own to be sorted out. May was exhausted, her nerves shattered, and she did not want to hear any more talk of hospitals. The following day, the journalist Saïd Freiha requested a meeting with her for an interview. May agreed, and told him everything. The interview was like a bomb exploding: readers in Lebanon were appalled to learn what had happened to her. The Egyptian press picked up the article. From then on, apology articles came raining down: everyone wanted to perform their personal *mea culpa*.

May spent three weeks in the American hospital. The number of her file, 2876, became her new identity. Her ordeal was coming to an end.

At the end of January, at Joseph's request, the Minister of Health decreed that May should be examined by a team of doctors to establish her mental state.

A week later, the team of doctors, who had come several times to examine May, delivered a four-page report in her favour. The doctors said that they had no objection to her transfer. They simply asked that she have a live-in nurse, and be closely monitored by a specialist.

On 8th February, the minister agreed to the transfer. On the 14th, May left hospital.

Prince Khaled Al-Jazairi had found her a nice little furnished house in the Ras Beirut neighbourhood, where she would be able to live with her loyal friend and nurse Esther Wakim. It was a pretty house with a red-tiled roof and a charming garden where, when the weather was mild, she could spend her evenings watching the sunset.

Before long, the house became a haven where all of the authors and intellectuals of the day would get together. May spent many peaceful moments there. But the legal battle to take back her rights and her money, and finally be rid of Joseph's guardianship, was still not over.

The cousins were not going to let her get away from them like that: they tried to launch another case against her to keep her under guardianship.

All of her friends were furious but May, on the contrary, was delighted: her cousins had just handed her proof that they had persecuted her and that they were continuing to do so. As for Rihani, without letting May know what he was doing, he had sent letters to all of her old friends in Cairo, telling them the truth about what had happened and the battle May was fighting. Some of them made the journey to come and see her, but May refused to see them. Lutfi El-Sayed wrote to her: she did not write back. Not to him, and not to Taha either: they had defended women's rights and freedom, but when their own friend, May herself, had been a victim of patriarchal oppression, they hadn't lifted a finger to defend her.

Huda Shaarawi sent a long letter, too, and it was the only one that May answered: she sent a postcard with a picture of a field of forget-me-nots signed, 'To my friend Huda. May'.

May's lawyers were not happy with the way the court case was developing: the lead judge was young and inexperienced, and he did not know the case well enough. Nor did he know Arab literature well enough to understand the role May had played in its renaissance. The court asked for a hearing with May. Her lawyers knew full well that she would never agree to go, and so they decided to explain to her, with the help of her friends, that the best way of convincing the judges was to agree to give a lecture to which they would all be invited.

They suggested the idea to her, and to their great surprise, May agreed. Hbeich proposed that his literary association al-Urwa al-Wuthqa (The Unbreakable Bond) organise the lecture for 22nd March, and that it take place at the American University in Beirut.

For three weeks, May worked on her talk, a lecture titled 'Risalat al-Adab ila al-Mujtama' (A Letter from Literature to Society).

The momentous day arrived. May was escorted by bodyguards that her friends had insisted on sending her for her protection. Her friends did not trust her cousins at all, and were afraid they would launch a physical attack on May. She said to them, 'When did you all become so paranoid?'

May went in through the artists' entrance. The room was full to bursting. Judges, lawyers, the public prosecutor, celebrities, intellectuals, journalists, students, doctors, they had all come to listen to May.

One of the organisers of the event, Kanaan Khatib, wanted to check with May that she was ready and that she had her text with her. He offered to take care of her notes himself so that they would be at hand when she was onstage; he could bring them to her if necessary. May realised straight away what was going on, and replied that she had no notes and had never needed any. She looked at him and said: 'It's all in here', pointing to her head. She saw the panic on his face, and it made her smile. Then she said to him: 'You too, Brutus?' Next the Egyptian consul came into her dressing room without permission. He greeted her and congratulated her on her return to cultural life. She replied drily:

'Thank you for your kind attention. You can see yourself out'. He was most offended and kept insisting:

'But I'm the Egyptian consul!'

V

Unmoved, she simply asked him politely to go and join the audience.

That night, May wore a black dress. Simple yet elegant. Her hair, now white from the time she had spent in the asylum, was tied back with a black ribbon. She walked out onto the stage and stopped for a moment to look at all the people who had come. It made her feel dizzy. Wherever she looked, there were faces staring at her. There was a deep silence for a few seconds, that seemed to her to go on for years. Then the applause began, a sublime ovation in her honour. At that moment, May remembered the speech she had given in Cairo, in honour of Gibran. She remembered that, to overcome her nerves, she had drawn on the love she felt for him. Her thoughts flew to him in that moment. To her Gibran.

May waited for the room to calm down, for the applause to finish and for silence to fall, and then she walked over to the lectern.

She was silent for a moment. The room was thick with tension, and with the fear that May would not be able to hold back her emotions.

May started to speak. For an hour her words poured out, reverberating throughout the room, reaching the hearts of her audience. When she finished, the room erupted. Applause came raining down. May left the stage. Everyone was wild with excitement, their joy to see her among them was indescribable. They cried out: 'May, you're back, we're here for you!'

A young man came up to her and said:

'I just wanted to tell you that I aspire to being as mad as you, dear May'.

May looked at him. Seeing how young he was, she answered him in an Egyptian dialect: 'Lessa badri', there's still time.

The lecture was a roaring success, it made all the newspapers. Many of them transcribed the entire thing, and *al-Makchouf* even published a front-page portrait of May painted by the great artist Youssef Howayek.

After the lecture, the court did not reach a decision immediately. There were still several more weeks of waiting. The session took place in the courthouse. It was a public hearing, and the room was full.

The lawyers of both parties spoke. Each one presented their case in turn. Then it was down to the public prosecutor to give his verdict. He began by saying that he might, at first, have had his doubts, but that after the public lecture he no longer had any uncertainty about May's mental state. Having witnessed her ability to prepare a speech like that, and the way in which she had delivered it to such a huge audience ...

'How could anyone have said that she was mad?' he asked. 'We are the mad ones. If she is mad, then we are madder still. That lecture was incontrovertible proof that her so-called madness was a fabrication. May must not be put under guardianship. She must not have her freedom taken from her. She must be left in peace to live with her real family, those who were cheering for her at the end of her lecture. To put her under guardianship would be to put all of Arab literature under guardianship'.

Before reaching their verdict, the members of the jury wanted to see May. They went to see her at her home, where she welcomed them with all the calm that she could muster. At the end of their visit, they left her house convinced that she had been the victim of a great injustice. But even after this response, the court was obliged once again to give in to the demands of her cousins and submit May to yet another medical examination. May refused: she did not want to suffer such humiliation again. Her friends did not know what to do to convince her to change her mind. When Dr Calmet, who was the one assigned to examine her, came to visit her without warning, May told Esther to ask him to leave the house.

May's friends felt helpless, and turned to Rihani who, after the session at the courthouse, had thought that things were definitively settled and had gone back to his village, Freike. And so Rihani sent a letter to May begging her to endure these examinations one last time, telling her that her smile and her intelligence had to win through.

After the medical examination finally took place, and they had read through a whole series of reports, the doctors gave a favourable opinion once more. The court finally announced its verdict: on 1st June 1938, it dismissed the request to keep May under guardianship.

That day, justice was done. May was free.

One afternoon, May received a visit from Wadadd Ghantous. She was the headmistress of Ahliah School, a prestigious school for girls in Beirut. She said to May: 'Our girls need you, they need your words, your strength. I want them to learn from you how to fight against oppression'.

May accepted the invitation immediately.

Full of apprehension, she went to the school on the agreed day.

The classroom was full. May saw the faces of all the girls looking up at her with undivided attention. It was like a reward for all she had been through. Now she knew what she had to do: she had to inspire in these girls the desire to continue the fight.

May had prepared a special speech for the occasion. It was based on a text she had written for a lecture she gave in 1921, 'Life's Purpose', in which she described a dream she had had:

'I had a dream that women, all women, will hold their heads high, that women will work, that in their eyes we will no longer see fear or defeat or humiliation. That women will never again be shackled by society, or by circumstance, or by men. Instead we will see in the eyes of every woman a person fully in control of herself, and mistress of her own destiny.

'I dreamt of a new birth, a new existence, the new woman.

'Today, girls, I am calling on you to make this dream a reality'.

May thought that things would happen quickly and that soon she would be able to go back to Egypt, even if she was furious with her friends in Cairo, and especially with the people at *al-Ahram*, whom she had considered family for such a long time. And yet they were the ones who had handed over her apartment to her cousins. The newspaper owned that apartment; she had rented it from them. They could have refused to hand it over, and waited for her to return. Instead, they had given it to her cousins who at that very moment were in the process of compiling a case against her to put her under guardianship there, in Cairo.

VI

The next day, at dawn, May was sitting on her terrace in Freike, looking out over the mountain and the valley. She saw Gibran's face smiling at her. This was his place, these were his mountains and valleys, and in the quiet of her soul, she spoke to him:

'It's only now that I understand why you were so insistent that I should write with my own emotions and stop talking about the lives of others. My dear Gibran, that's what I'm going to do. You will be by my side in this new adventure, you're the one who will give me the strength I need'.

That summer, May spent unforgettable moments with Rihani, strolling together through the streets of the village, the same paths they had walked together in 1911. They liked to go as far as the last house in the village, the furthest one ...

It was always empty. They would climb up to the roof terrace and watch the sun set over the valley and over the Mediterranean, just visible in the distance.

May lived in that village for four months. She felt so happy there that she would prepare meals for everyone and sing for her friends in the evenings. May and Rihani spent much of their time reading, writing and talking. She confided in him that she was working on two books. One of them was about the friends who stood by her through the tragedy she had endured, and that she had called *The Saviours*; the other would be a book entitled *Nights in the Asylum*. 'And that's where I'm going to tell the whole story about my time in Asfourieh. You'll see, my dear Rihani, you'll be the first to read it'. Telling the story was the only way that May could get over the hell she had lived through. She nursed the hope that her experience would serve as a lesson, that such a tragedy would not occur again.

Even though Esther had hidden all the newspapers, one day May discovered on the front page of the Egyptian papers: 'The king is dead, long live the king!' While she had been in the asylum, a new king had taken the throne in Egypt. King Fuad had died some time after she had left Egypt, and now Farouk was on the throne. She learned in the same newspaper that many of her old friends had become ministers and high-ranking people ... The pain of their betrayal came flooding back to her. She spoke about it at length with Rihani, but the bitterness and indignation did not dissipate. Why hadn't a single one of them defended her? Had they forgotten all the battles she had fought in their name in the pages of *al-Mahrousa*?

All of her friends in Lebanon were working actively so that May could return to Cairo at the end of the summer. The legal battle in Egypt was going to be tough. The cousins were determined to put May under guardianship in Cairo, and they had the support of the Egyptian consul in Lebanon.

May's lawyers had sent the full case file of the court hearing in Lebanon, along with the reports and the verdict, thinking that that would be enough to win the case in Egypt.

Khalil Thabet, the owner of the *al-Muqattam* newspaper and one of May's old friends, was designated as her official guardian by the Religious and Legal High Council. This sent her into a blind rage: how could he have accepted such a thing? She would never be able to forgive him for such a betrayal.

At the same time, Rihani sent a letter to the Minister of Religious Affairs, Mustafa Abdel Razek, who was also an old friend of May's, to ask for his help. Abdel Razek did everything in his power to help them lift the guardianship, but his efforts were in vain. So he sent a letter to Rihani, advising him to take the matter to court because the Religious and Legal High Council had more power than his ministry. The High Council had allocated May a monthly stipend of fifty Egyptian pounds. May felt deeply humiliated by the whole thing.

And to make things even more unbearable, May had to undergo yet another medical examination for the court case in Egypt. In an attempt to try to avoid this new affront, her friends asked the doctors who had written the first report just to write another. They told them that May had gained twenty kilos while she was in Freike, that she was well and that she had started writing again. And so the doctors of the Commission wrote up their report without having seen or examined May. A report that was, of course, in her favour. Like everyone else, they had no doubt that she was of sound mind.

Fares al-Khoury, a friend of May's, had found out that Hussein Idris Bey, Grand Master of the Religious and Legal High Council in Cairo, was spending his holidays in Chtoura, in Lebanon. He went with him to keep him company, and to visit Rihani and May in Freike. He came to meet them with Idris and his wife before they went back to Cairo. They spent one of the most glorious days of the whole summer together; many friends were there and they had prepared a grand barbecue for their guests. At the end of the day, Idris and his wife thanked them for what had been one of the most wonderful days of their holiday. Idris assured them that he would do everything in his power to help them. The last sentence he uttered before they left was, 'This injustice must end'.

Everyone hoped that at the start of the autumn the whole affair would finally be over and that May would be able to get a new Egyptian passport – hers had expired a long time ago.

Rihani decided to delay his return to the USA to stay with May in Freike. The cold weather would soon come, and May's friends were increasingly worried at the thought of her being on her own.

One day, a well-known writer named Maroun Abboud asked May to give a talk at a conference that was being organised in honour of Gibran. As soon as May heard Gibran's name, her tears began and she turned down the invitation: 'I couldn't possibly speak of him in public. It's too hard for me, I still can't bring myself to do it'. She always kept Gibran's precious letters with her and, when she missed his love too dearly, she would shut herself away with his letters to read and reread them.

At the start of December 1938, Rihani was obliged to return to the USA. Everything was ready for his departure, except for May. Saying goodbye to Rihani was extremely difficult for her, and heartbreaking for the others to witness. They were all devastated to see her so sad and broken. They tried to reassure her that Rihani would be back the following summer and that he would come to see her in Cairo, but it made no difference: May needed him now. She was afraid that she would never see him again.

The al-Urwa al-Wuthqa association invited May to give another lecture at the American University of Beirut. She liked the idea of meeting the people of Beirut one last time before she left. A very special evening was in store for her. May was greeted with a wave of applause, and she spoke to the students about their responsibility for the future and for the progress of their country. At the end of her speech, which had lasted almost an hour and a quarter, the audience began to shout, 'Long live May, long live the greatest of all Arab authors!'

After that evening, May stayed with friends, biding her time until the long-awaited moment of her return to Cairo. But she realised that the situation with her cousins would never be resolved if she did not go and see to it herself. She told her friends that she had decided to go back to Cairo as soon as possible. They agreed that it was the right decision, especially since she had finally received her new Egyptian passport.

She decided to travel by boat, in memory of the journey she had once made with her father. She told herself: 'He'll be there by my side, we'll make this journey together and we'll look out at the sea once more'.

In the weeks leading up to her departure, May had some unforgettable times. She loved the Al-Jazairis' daughters as if they were her own children, and so one evening, she gave them the gift of playing an air on the piano just for them.

Two days before she left, Prince Khaled Al-Jazairi threw a big party in May's honour. It gave her the opportunity to say goodbye to all her friends, and to gather them all around her one last time. It was a spectacular party, with food, dancing and singing. Everyone was smiling, happy to see May in good health. When the evening was drawing to a close, Prince Khaled gave a short speech, in which he made a revelation that completely bowled May over:

'My brother and I have decided that our wives, who are like sisters to you, will accompany you on your journey to Cairo. Their cabin is already reserved on the same boat as you, and they will stay with you until you are settled in an apartment of your own'.

May got up to embrace them and thank them, but instead of words, it was tears that flowed to express her joy and her gratitude.

She said to them over and over: 'Don't be alarmed, they're tears of joy'.

*

At the start of January 1939, May was waiting on the quay at the port of Beirut. It was midday and she was accompanied by all her friends, who had come to wave her off as she left.

From the deck, May watched the shore getting further and further away. Soon Beirut was nothing more than a black dot on the horizon. Rain and fog obscured the landscape, making it seem even more melancholic. May sensed that it was the last time she would see Beirut, that this view of her country would be her last. Hot tears rolled down her cheeks. As the boat set sail, through the fog she could see Esther's face, Esther, that wonderful friend who had taken such great care of her. In her mind's eye she saw herself back with Esther, sitting on the bench in the garden at Asfourieh. She remembered Esther carving her name, 'May', as a permanent reminder of her time there. She could still hear Esther's voice saying to her: 'When you get out of here and I have no one to sit beside, I'll come here and I'll look at your name, and I'll think of you, dear friend'.

A few days later, the boat docked at the port of Alexandria. May remembered all the times she had arrived at this port with her parents. She missed them terribly. As she and her friends were preparing to get off the boat, she studied the quay to see whether her old friends from Cairo had come to give her a surprise welcome. But nothing, not a single familiar face. However, Felix Fares and his wife were waiting for them. Prince Khaled had sent word to Felix to announce their arrival and asking him to go and meet them. Felix and his wife were old friends of theirs; they were charming and attentive. They accompanied the three women until the moment they dropped them off at the station in Alexandria to take the train to Cairo.

As soon as they arrived, Salma and Zahra Al-Jazairi and May began their search for an apartment. They wanted to get the job done as soon as possible so that Salma and Zahra could return to Lebanon and to their families.

They had reserved rooms in a small hotel in the city centre, one that matched May's modest budget. While they were eating their breakfast, May picked up the *al-Ahram* newspaper to read. All she found were two insignificant lines announcing 'the return of Miss May'. It was the only newspaper in Cairo that had even mentioned it. May could not believe her eyes. She looked at her friends and said to them:

'Oh dear God, what life is this! This is how the Egyptian press welcomes me back! *Al-Ahram* no less! I gave this newspaper the best years of my life, the best texts I ever wrote. I contributed to its development for years, and this is the reception I get! They even had the cheek to say that intellectuals and public figures were at the port to greet me. Really? I looked everywhere and I didn't see a soul, where were they hiding? Where was Gemayel, where was Moutran? Where were Taha Hussein, Akkad and Lutfi, and ...'.

She tried in vain to hold back her tears, but the pain was too great.

Felix and his wife joined forces with May and her friends to help them in their search. A few days later, they managed to find her an apartment in a block of flats at 16 El Sabaa Street. May finally had a place of her own.

Before they left the hotel, they were visited by Hussein Idris, the Grand Master of the Religious and Legal High Council. He was the one May had had the pleasure of meeting when he and his wife had come to Freike in the summer. His wife had also come with him to the hotel bar. He explained to May how things were proceeding with the court case, and congratulated her on her decision to return because, he said, that would help to move things along.

May had settled well into her new apartment, which she soon got into the habit of calling 'my den'. Her friends stayed with her for another fortnight, just the time that was needed to get her settled in and be sure she was comfortable. They were even more reassured because Idris and his wife were always close at hand.

After the Al-Jazairis had left, Idris and his wife asked May if they could bring a couple of friends by to see her. At the end of the afternoon, they arrived with Mustafa Merii and his wife Nour. They were a delightful couple. Mustafa was an intellectual and had long admired May's work. They had a lovely time talking about literature and politics, even if, since the tragedy that had befallen her, May no longer had the patience to follow current affairs. When they left, May insisted that they must come back to see her again.

And so Mustafa and Nour started to come and see her more and more often, sometimes with Idris and sometimes just the two of them. They talked about poetry, Sufism, literature, politics. Sometimes they discussed the explosive situation the world was in. They were convinced that a second world war would break out.

May kept saying: 'I'm going to have the honour of living through two world wars in a single lifetime'. They would also tell each other about their memories, about the past and the things they cared about. May spent the majority of her time with these two couples, as if she had always known them. They became her new family.

One evening, Idris invited them all to dine at Manshiyet al-Bakri, a very fashionable restaurant. They talked about this and that. But May could not manage to hide how sad she felt because *al-Mahrousa* had just been closed down. Mustafa said to her: 'Why don't you pick up the torch? It's your newspaper, you can do what you want with it!' May's eyes lit up. She saw herself back in her father's office during the glory years, she could hear the voices, the discussions, the laughter ... She wanted to believe that she could relive all of that: 'But how would I go about that?' she asked. Mustafa replied: 'It's simple: if you give power of attorney to a friend of mine, who is one of Cairo's greatest lawyers, he'll do the necessary. And if handing over to a lawyer worries you, make the power of attorney over to me, and I'll deal with the rest'. May agreed to the proposal straight away. The next day, Mustafa came by with a clerk and May gave him power of attorney.

On 19th February 1939, while Nour was at May's house, there was a loud knock on the door. Nour ran to open it and see who it could be. Mustafa came in and, barging straight past her, started talking to May:

'My dear May, I have to tell you something I've been keeping from you, and I hope you will forgive me. I'll tell you everything as long as you promise to let me say it all without interrupting me'.

May agreed. He looked her straight in the eyes, and said:

'I'm a lawyer ... One day last January, my friend Hussein Idris came to see me. He asked me to defend you in court, and gave me the whole case file with all the necessary documents for the trial, including the reports and verdicts from Lebanon. He explained that he had known nothing about what you had been through and that, when your cousins came to see him at the High Council to petition for you to be put under guardianship, at first he had believed their lies and had authorised the guardianship. Over the summer, while Idris was with his family in Lebanon, Ameen Rihani and Fares al-Khoury invited him to come and meet you, so that he could see with his own eyes the lies that had been spread about you. He told me that the day he spent in Freike with his wife had been one of the most wonderful and enriching days of his whole holiday. When he left Freike, he was consumed with guilt: it was because of him that you had had to carry on living with this injustice and that you had been fighting for months. He swore that he would do all he could to get you out of there. He came and sought me out and said to me: "My friend May Ziadeh is an exceptional woman, one of the greatest writers of our time. She deserves to be given back her honour, which her cousins have violated, and she deserves our deepest love and greatest respect. Defending May is the duty of every free being, and you, my friend, are the one best placed to do it. But things aren't as simple as I've set them out to you; the hardest thing of all will be to convince May to hand over power of attorney to a lawyer, or even just to agree to meet with a lawyer. I have a suggestion: we'll go to see her, and I'll introduce you as my friend, an admirer of her work, and we'll find a way to get her to sign a power of attorney for you". I accepted the mission straight away. The power of attorney that I got you to sign was for me, so that I could defend you in court and have your guardianship overturned. And that's what I've just done, just now'.

He stared at her intently and saw that May hadn't yet grasped what he was telling her. And so, with an enormous smile, and his eyes brimming with pride and with tears, he said to her:

'My dear May, I have the honour of telling you that you have just won your case. You are as free as the air. Forgive me for lying to you, it was only to help you'.

May began to cry: after so many years, finally she had won, finally she was free!

She said to her friend: 'You completely fooled me, my dear Mustafa. You did it, you played your role perfectly. Oh how I wish all my defeats could be like this one! The glorious defeat of victory'.

From that day on, they were inseparable. May took back possession of what was rightfully hers. She was very sad to see the state in which her things had been left, and she was particularly sad about the loss of her first oud, the one she had bought in Damascus. Most of her belongings had disappeared.

Idris and May sent letters to all their friends to let them know the good news. May wrote letters of thanks, enclosing a cheque with each one to return all the money she had borrowed. She was delighted to at least be able to give back the money they had lent her. Letters of congratulations came flowing in. Rihani was over the moon.

Even though she did not return to the *al-Mahrousa* offices, she followed the relaunch closely. She also wrote a number of articles that were published in the newspaper *al-Hilal*. She even agreed to give a lecture at the American University of Cairo entitled 'Towards a Social Culture'.

On 15th January 1940, May gave her first lecture since her return to Egypt. She received a very warm welcome and that day she wore black, as she had done ever since she arrived back in Cairo, with a matching narrow ribbon tying back her white hair.

One day, her friend Kanaan came from Lebanon to visit her in Cairo. May invited him to dinner at Chez al-Hani, a little restaurant renowned for its delicious food. She kept apologising for the strange way she had to go about eating, because of her teeth. When he told her not to worry about it, May replied:

'You know, dear friend, I'm just happy to have got out of the asylum with only my teeth broken'.

They ended the evening at the cinema, and then Kanaan accompanied her home. They strolled together through the streets of Cairo, just as May and her father used to do when returning home late at night, after a long day at work. The next day, she invited him to come for tea and to meet her friends Idris and the Merïis. They finished the evening as they always did, singing together.

Kanaan was delighted to see her surrounded by such good friends. Before he returned to Lebanon, he went to see his friend Taha Hussein and told him about the pleasant times he had spent with May in those last few days. Taha took May's number and plucked up the courage to call her; he had been too afraid to do so since her return.

The telephone rang. May answered and heard Taha's voice at the other end of the line, saying to her:

'My dear May, our friend Kanaan told me that he has just had the most wonderful time with you. I thought you were still ill and tired. Now that I know you're well again, I'd very much like to come and see you. Tell me when I can come, dear May'.

She answered him simply:

'No, Mr Hussein. When I was locked away in the hospitals of Beirut, you didn't even think of calling me or asking after me. Not you, not Gemayel, not Moutran, not Akkad, not Lutfi El-Sayed. And so now I say to you: No. No thank you'.

After all these betrayals, there was nothing left of her former life except Rihani. But fate was determined to take everyone she loved away from her. Rihani was killed when a car hit him in his village, Freike, on one of the roads they had walked together. The most banal death imaginable, and so all the more cruel for May. The Orient had just lost a great man.

One day, May received an invitation from the Orientalist Charles Adams to give a lecture at the American University in Cairo. Her friends encouraged her to accept. Despite her sorrow, eventually she accepted the invitation and channelled all the energy and passion she had left into writing the lecture. She gave it the title 'Live Dangerously'.

On 20th January 1941, May gave what would be her final lecture, in front of a packed audience that received her with great ceremony. At the end of her lecture, the students went wild and called out her name, she could hear everywhere cries of 'Long live May!'

A few months later, sitting on her bed, she felt her breath grow weak ... she struggled to breathe. Her body was failing her. She found the strength to write the final words of her book: 'I am free'.

On 19th October 1941, May Ziadeh passed away at El Maadi hospital, in Cairo. She was 55 years old. On her tomb is written:

'Here lies May Ziadeh, genius of the Orient, leader of the Arab Renaissance, literary and social icon. Pray for her soul'.

VII

My dear May,

In the end you won. People are still talking about you, your work and your story. I tell snippets of your life in my play. Every evening I call out your name, I talk to you, I tell people about your struggles, and Huda's. And every evening people come up to ask me questions about you, about the woman who saved my life. And I answer with great pride.

While I was doing my research, I travelled back and forth between Paris and Cairo. I couldn't find any of the places you used to frequent. Everything has changed, even the names of the streets. I asked passersby for help. Every time they would direct me to the oldest person in the neighbourhood to guide me. None of your apartments has survived. The last building you lived in with your parents, in the apartment that belonged to the *al-Ahram* newspaper, no longer exists. In its place is a big open-air carpark.

The Café Riche is still there, though. It almost got shut down, but as luck would have it, it was saved. On the inside, there were still some traces of times past. I was incredibly moved to see all the photos and portraits of the people who had been regular patrons of the café and had contributed to its fame: Taha, Lutfi, Zaghloul. Abdel Wahab was there, too, and the great Sayed Darwish, and of course there was an enormous canvas of Umm Kulthum.

'Wasn't there a theatre here once?' I asked the waiter.

'You should ask Ammo Felfel, Uncle Felfel, he's the one who's been around here the longest'.

Felfel was an old Sudanese man who never stopped smiling. He talked and talked, telling me all his memories of the café since he had started working there in 1942. He didn't get to meet you, but he pointed to the building right next door to the café and said to me, 'That's where the theatre was'. And just beside it I found the

Groppi café. It's still there, in the same place with the same sign above the door, but the clientele and the ambience are nothing like they were when you used to go there, and you can't drink alcohol at the Groppi any more …

There was only one place left for me to visit: the cemetery where you are laid to rest. When I got there, the warden greeted me with a smile.

'May Ziadeh, please', I said.

And straight away he answered:

'Oh yes, the great writer! Follow me, madam. I'll take you to her'.

Finally I got to visit you! I followed the guardian through the tombstones. We went towards the columbarium wall. He said to me:

'There you go, this is where she is laid to rest!'

A drawer!

I had heard that you had a tomb covered with flowers … I had tears in my eyes. The guardian tried to console me and apologised as if it were his fault:

'Are you a member of the family?'

I shook my head.

'You know, madam, many families moved away and a lot of the occupants of the tombs here haven't had any visitors for decades. So we give their spot to the new arrivals and the older ones get moved to the columbarium drawers. It's nothing against Miss May – even the owner of the cemetery is in a drawer, right next to hers! Don't be sad, she's in good company. Wasn't this one a friend of hers?'

He pointed to a niche just above yours. Guess who was laid to rest there? Your old friend Gemayel, the one who betrayed you and who you never forgave. Life does play some tricks on us, my dear May!

The warden looked at me and asked:

'Are you Lebanese?'

I told him I was.

And he said:

'Could you do something for me, and go to visit someone else while you're here? No one has been to see her for a long time, and I think she'd like that'.

He led me through the tombstones again, and we arrived at the other columbarium. And there I was in front of the resting place of the great singer, Laure Daccache. I stayed with her for a little while, and then I came back to you. I needed to talk to you, to tell you things I've never dared tell anyone but you.

My dearest May,

Every morning I walk along the banks of the Seine. I walk as far as the hotel you stayed in, on the Quai Voltaire. I look out at the river, 'our Nile', as you used to call it. As I walk, I can still hear your voice singing 'Ya Hanaina', your favourite song. I turn around and I can see your smiling face, just as I saw you that first evening in the asylum, when you came to me. Since then, your face and your smile have never left me. You are by my side and we walk together, hand in hand.

I am no longer alone.

Acknowledgements

Darina Al Joundi would like to thank the following for their support: Salma Haffar Kozbari, Marjorie, Danielle Domino, Anaïs Fiammetta, Christophe, Caroline, Pierre, Claude.

Translator's note

Though *Prisoner of the Levant* is presented as a biography – the subtitle that appears on the jacket of the original 2017 French publication, 'La vie méconnue de May Ziadé' (The Little-Known Life of May Ziadeh), indicates a work of non-fiction – it is a more creative and personal piece than this would suggest. Its primary focus is not May's literary career and prestige, but instead her personal awakenings and sufferings. In particular, we learn about her intense epistolary relationship with Khalil Gibran, her growing awareness of women's inequality, and the brutal repression she herself suffered at the hands of the men in her family when she was left unprotected after her father's death.

May Ziadeh's story is deeply imbricated with Al Joundi's own. In the final chapter of *Prisoner of the Levant*, Al Joundi refers to May as 'the woman who saved my life', and the resonance between the two women's lives – separated by almost exactly eighty-two years – is striking. Both are celebrated as pioneers of women's emancipation through their artistic careers and refusal to conform to stereotypical expectations of 'domesticated' femininity, and both were raised in progressive and relatively affluent households. Yet when the death of a protector befell both May and Darina, all their freedom and privilege was revealed to be an illusion. The men in the family took over to do their 'duty' (in Darina's case, to 'correct' her behaviour; in May's, to take charge of her wealth and estate) by condemning them to a fallacious – and, because of the legal subjugation of women, incontestable – diagnosis of madness.

In her homage to May Ziadeh, Al Joundi writes that she mentions May in her play every time she performs it. The play Al Joundi is referring to here is her one-woman monologue *Ma Marseillaise* (*Marseillaise My Way*), the sequel to her critically acclaimed first play *Le jour où Nina Simone a cessé de chanter* (*The Day Nina Simone Stopped Singing*).[1] In these plays, Al Joundi performs as Noun, a character whose life mirrors her own. Growing up in Beirut during the Lebanese civil war with a 'devoutly secular' father, Noun's ideals of freedom are brutally restricted when, like May, she is forcibly sedated, straightjacketed and incarcerated in an asylum at the behest of her family. *Marseillaise My Way* follows Noun as she starts a new life in the West after her release, and in it Noun invokes May, calling out to her and drawing strength from her resilience in order to overcome her own challenges. In the final chapter of *Prisoner of the Levant*, Al Joundi reiterates how this deep connection with May lifted her out of solitude – a solidarity that she reciprocates by giving voice to May's own struggles in this work.

As part of this recovery of May's voice and experience, Al Joundi undertook extensive research to be able to write – and do justice to – May's story. This results in references to a vast range of places, people and organisations, as May's experience was complex, and connected to numerous individuals and institutions both in her glory days and in her darkest hours. I have reproduced these as frugally as possible in the translation, so that they offer some minor clarification of context without impeding the communication of the story itself. There are instances, however, where additional detail would have represented too great an intervention. For example, the name of the asylum, Asfourieh, sometimes appears in inverted commas in the original text and sometimes without. Asfourieh was the first psychiatric hospital in Beirut, and has now become popularised as a term synonymous with any asylum (in a manner comparable to the use of 'bedlam' in English). The inverted commas indicate this dual meaning, but reproducing them in the translation would not be sufficient to indicate this distinction in an anglophone context, and so I have kept the focus on Asfourieh as a proper noun rather than as a general term.

There are also occasional cross-references to people, events or circumstances that might not previously have been mentioned; where possible, I have sketched in connections so that the continuity of the narrative is not disrupted. Where this could not

---

1   Both plays were published in French by Avant-scène théâtre in 2012, and in my translation by Naked Eye Publishing in 2022.

be done without significant additions or assumptions, I have left the references as they are. Hence there is occasional ambiguity: for example, May's dream of building a house in Chahtoul is referenced shortly afterwards as a concrete project forestalled by her authoritarian cousins, and Chapter VI opens with May on the terrace of her house in Freike, though the only accommodation we have seen her rent at this point is a house in Ras Beirut. Similarly, after May's release from the asylum she makes out a number of cheques once her wealth has been returned to her, though we had not previously known that she had depended on financial assistance or who her benefactors were. Any attempt to offer a transition between these references would have altered the original text, and so I have limited my intervention to offering as much precision as possible within the context of the information available.

Although the genre and style of *Prisoner of the Levant* differ from Al Joundi's plays, there are nonetheless recognisable characteristics that trace connections between them. In particular, the boundaries between fact and fiction are blurred: whereas the fictional narrator of Al Joundi's plays recounts experiences that are based on Al Joundi's own, *Prisoner of the Levant* is perhaps best described as a fictional biography. It does not pretend to offer a full account of May's life, but rather focuses on periods of her life and aspects of her experience that are most meaningful to Al Joundi, prioritising May as a person rather than as a writer. Here as elsewhere, Al Joundi favours short sentences, and has a remarkable ability to evoke a place or a situation in the most economical terms. I have endeavoured to respect this in the translation, condensing narrative description where possible. In instances where no single word or short phrase maps neatly onto the original, I have instead included two brief clauses or sentences so that the work remains representative of Al Joundi's writing style without sacrificing the multiple meanings and implications of the original text. Another common feature of Al Joundi's writing – both here and in her plays – is the matter-of-fact way in which she describes horrific events. There is no gratuitous melodrama: the brutality inflicted on women is presented unembellished, and so I have aimed for the same minimalist approach in the translation.

The first and last chapters, in which Al Joundi offers a more personal insight into her relationship with May Ziadeh's life and legacy, fall somewhere between the style of *The Day Nina Simone*

Stopped Singing/Marseillaise My Way and the bulk of *Prisoner of the Levant*. Though never self-indulgent – and always careful to keep her focus determinedly on May – these chapters underline the intensely personal investment that Al Joundi has in writing this story of May's life, and in raising her out of the silence inflicted on her. This translation of *Prisoner of the Levant* into English extends Al Joundi's commitment to fighting back against people and customs that deny women their autonomy, to bearing witness to those who have suffered at the hands of these people and customs, and to ensuring that May's legacy endures.